COMMON UTTERANCES OF THE MALE LIE-BIDO

To Women:

"I'll call you this week."

"Me married? Whatever gave you that idea?"

"I'm not dating anyone else."

"This is your daughter? I thought you were sisters."

"Your mother is a great lady!"

"Did anyone ever tell you how cute you are when you're asleep?"

"I promise to love, cherish, and obey."

To Men:

"Yeah, I know I look tired. Must've been those sixteen-year-old twins."

"Just like Christie Brinkley, only bigger boobs."

"So I said, 'Honey, please, I have to go to work.'"

"After I was through, she wanted to pay me."

DAVID A. RUDNITSKY is a slightly insecure writer who will often ask lovers in the morning, "Was it good for me, too?"

MEN WHO HATE THEMSELVES*

by

David A. Rudnitsky

Illustrations by
Bob Trondsen

*And the Women Who Agree with Them

A PLUME BOOK

NEW AMERICAN LIBRARY

A DIVISION OF PENGUIN BOOKS USA INC., NEW YORK
PUBLISHED IN CANADA BY
PENGUIN BOOKS CANADA LIMITED, MARKHAM, ONTARIO

Dedicated to Abigail B. Wright

Whose insights, patience and vision contributed so greatly to this book. And who also wanted me to go on a Vision Quest, which I did, discovering my contact lenses exactly where I left them.

NAL BOOKS ARE AVAILABLE AT QUANTITY DISCOUNTS WHEN USED TO PROMOTE PRODUCTS OR SERVICES. FOR INFORMATION PLEASE WRITE TO PREMIUM MARKETING DIVISION, NEW AMERICAN LIBRARY, 1633 BROADWAY, NEW YORK, NEW YORK 10019.

Published simultaneously in Canada by Penguin Books Canada Limited

PLUME TRADEMARK REG. U.S. PAT. OFF. AND FOREIGN COUNTRIES
REGISTERED TRADEMARK—MARCA REGISTRADA
HECHO EN DRESDEN, TN, U.S.A.

SIGNET, SIGNET CLASSIC, MENTOR, ONYX, PLUME, MERIDIAN and NAL BOOKS are published *in the United States* by New American Library, a division of Penguin Books USA Inc., 1633 Broadway, New York, New York 10019, *in Canada* by Penguin Books Canada Limited, 2801 John Street, Markham, Ontario L3R 1B4

First Printing, March, 1990

    2   3   4   5   6   7   8   9

PRINTED IN THE UNITED STATES OF AMERICA

TABLE OF CONTENTS

ACKNOWLEDGMENTS   ix

1: WOMEN WHO WRITE TOO MUCH   1

2: LOVE, MARRIAGE, AND PREMARITAL DIVORCE   8

3: EARLY ADOLESCENCE (THE DEFORMATIVE YEARS): AGES 6–81   21

4: MEN WHO SHOULD HATE THEMSELVES, BUT DON'T   30

5: GROVELING, PLEADING, WHINING, BEGGING, PLUS OTHER POPULAR SEXUAL POSITIONS   41

6: PROBING THE MALE LIE-BIDO   48

7: IMPERSONAL ADS   55

8: SAFE SEX IN THE EIGHTIES (OR HOW TO BE YOUR OWN BEST LOVER)—ADVICE FROM DR. BABY RUTH   62

9: DETERMINING A MAN'S H.Q. (HATE QUOTIENT)   69

10: LIVING, LOVING, AND LOATHING   78

11: PASSIVITY TRAINING FOR MEN   87

12: MEN WHO ARE THEIR OWN WORST ENEMY (AND OTHERS LESS FORTUNATE)   95

13: A DAY IN THE LIFE OF A MAN WHO
HATES HIMSELF   104

14: THE HATE REPORT (PLUS CHERI HATE'S
HATE MALE)   112

15: JANE FONDUE'S "AERO-PHOBICS FOR
MEN"   124

16: THE HIGH-SUGAR/LOW-ESTEEM DIET
(OR HOW TO COOK YOUR MAN'S GOOSE) 130

17: ZEN AND THE ART OF ANTIPATHY   136

18: MEN LEARNING TO LOVE TO HATE
THEMSELVES   142

CHARTS

MEN WHO HATE THEMSELVES . . .

By Size of Penis	13
By Favorite Rock Group	20
By Father's Occupation	23
By Country	29
By Exercises They Hate	47
By Exercises They Love	47
By Favorite Sexual Fantasy	53
By Girlfriend's Bra Size	61
By Visa Credit Limit	68
By College Major	77
By City	86
By Favorite Pet	94
By Favorite Movie	103
By Favorite Author	111
By First Name	123
By Wife's First Name	123
By Favorite Food	135

ACKNOWLEDGMENTS

First of all, I'd like to express my thanks to my editor, Michaela Hamilton, for her early enthusiasm about this project. Of course, what puzzles me is how such a lovely, intelligent, and otherwise delightful woman could possibly be drawn to such a weird idea. Oh well, the mysteries of life.

Next, I'd like to say how much I appreciate my agent, Frank Weimann, for laughing at just about everything, including his own shoe size. I have no idea what I mean by that.

Moving right along, I want to make special mention of some of the women who have affected me and therefore made this book a therapeutic reality. Unfortunately, they all swore they would severely damage several of my more sensitive areas if I used their full names. So special thanks to: DN, MM, ER, EK, EKG, OD, VD, LP, IUD, IRT, BMT, cc, KD, AW, CW, LG, CPA, BS, GD, HU, CH, IW (or WI, as she's known to her friends), AFL, CIO, BJ, OJ, JJ, KGB and, of course, PMS.

At this juncture, I'd also like to convey my gratitude to the folks at NAL, particularly Bob Diforio and Lisa Berkowitz, for their tireless efforts in support of my work. The same may be said for Maryann Palumbo, who also shares the honor (?) of having attended the very same high school as me.

In addition and very importantly, there are those in my funny family who are responsible for my sense of humor: my fabulous parents (who are actually more like my father and mother) Sam and Mollie, my cousin (who's actually more like my sister) Barbara, my Aunt (who's actually more like my daughter) Lilly, my Uncle (who's actually more like my uncle) Sidney, and of course Uncle Lou and Aunt Betty, either one of whom is quite capable of breaking me into tiny little amino acids if I didn't mention their names.

OK, I suppose I need a big funny finish right now. No sweat. Here it comes. Are you ready? What's that, Michaela? But I thought I had another three thousand words to—

MEN WHO HATE THEMSELVES*

CHAPTER 1

WOMEN WHO WRITE TOO MUCH

Across the country, wherever you go, from north to south, east to west, even outside Cleveland, more and more men are beginning to realize how much they hate themselves. Of course, for some, it required that their consciousness be raised with a tow truck, but for most others it was a natural outgrowth of the women's movement of the 60's, 70's and 80's. Indeed, before the Gloria Steinems and the Betty Friedans, most men never dreamt how selfish, petty, and hostile they really were.

Well, all this has changed. By 1993, sociologists predict almost all men will hate themselves. In fact, if current trends continue, only one man will be able to love himself by the year 1995 and that will be in Boise, Idaho, but unfortunately in public.

When you add up all the pages and all the books that have helped to teach men how vile and loathsome they really are, when you add up the collected works of Shere Hite, Robin Norwood, Germaine Greer, etc., you have over 7,885,612, 943,221,112,637 words that have been exclusively devoted to making men feel as if they were below the amoeba, the paramecium, or even some insurance agents on the evolutionary scale.

Contrast this to all the positive words these women have written about men and you will quickly see there have only been about eleven, and most of these have dealt with the superior ability that men exhibit when it comes to moving pianos.

SO JUST WHAT IS THE PROBLEM?

Clearly, the problem isn't Women Who Love Too Much, but Women Who *Write* Too Much, who are responsible for the millions of men who hate themselves today. However, should a man ever dare to articulate this point of view in public, just see how long it is before he's tarred, feathered, or even worse, forced to appear on the *Morton Downey Show*.

Why men never before realized what sleaze they really are is still a mystery. After all, there are countless reasons to hate oneself. A man can be too short, too tall, too fat, too thin; he can be losing his looks, the hair on his head, and even more traumatically, the hair on his chest. So when you look at the overall picture there are literally thousands of reasons for men to hate themselves.

Which brings us to another significant point. How many men can really find reasons to love themselves? Let's face it, even the historically strong points of the male animal have been turned into negatives by the women's movement.

Take for instance a stockbroker who occasionally works late, some weekends, and who only earns annually about $875,000 or so. Well, before you know it, his wife is accusing him of having tunnel vision, of being too "focused" on money and, therefore, not "sensitive" enough to her needs. So he quits his job, becomes a part-time librarian, and what do you know?

The very same woman accuses him of being a spineless wimp who'll never get ahead anyway and guess what. She winds up leaving him—for a Brooklyn bodybuilder!

Small wonder, from northern Maine to southern California, men are showing how much they hate themselves. They're letting out their feelings, as well as their pants, and what are they getting in return? Nothing, nothing but threats and accusations, warnings that they will lose the one thing they love more than anything else in the world, unless they pay their American Express bill.

Has anyone, anywhere, heard their cries for help? All they want is love, softness, compassion, and understanding, OK, maybe with a six-pack thrown in.

LET'S LOOK AT THE FACTS

The highest state a man can possibly reach today is "accepting" himself, which doesn't do most women any good since most of these guys are probably gay anyway. So what's the answer?

If current census figures are to be believed, there are exactly 125,834,917 men living in these United States today and even more, within the past fifty years, who have died. When you add these figures up there have been over 300 million men who have inhabited this nation at one time or another, many of whom had the good fortune to enjoy the unique benefits of male bonding, but mostly just to stay out of the army.

THE EVOLUTION OF MEN'S FEELINGS

In the year 234,879 B.C. (that's Before Consciousness), men were a pretty happy lot, content to eat brontosaurus burgers at their leisure. Clubs for men also existed, although these were frequently used to beat women into submission. But did we hear any complaints? Obviously not.

Moving along a few hundred thousand centuries we arrive at the end of the Bronze Age and at the start of the Age of Makeup. Perhaps the best-known figure of this time is Cleopatra, who seduced Marc Antony with her wit, charm, and Humphrey Bogart imitations, unconcerned all the while that she was tying up commercial barge traffic up and down the Nile.

A few hundred years later and the Romans are still having a grand old time conquering neighboring lands. They plunder, steal, rape, pillage, sell short. But instead of castigation and cries of misogyny from the various women's groups of the time, they are rewarded with laurel wreaths and weekend passes to Gaul.

Anyway, the Roman Empire ultimately falls, which ushers in the Dark Ages. Here again, even though all learning and civilization have practically disappeared, men are still pretty much a happy species, torturing heretics, fighting infidels, with occasional time off for burning witches and Monday Night Football.

Once more, do we hear any complaints from the women? Of course not. They're too busy treating plague victims to be bothered with petty issues like day care, abortion, and the inalienable right to pick up the check once in a while.

THE HISTORY OF WOMEN'S OPPRESSION OF MEN

The very first example of this, according to historical records, has to be Delilah, the cunning wench who cut off all of Samson's hair, even though he only came in for a light trim. Next are the Sirens of Greece, who decide, while at the beauty parlor, not only to drive men crazy with their song, but also to play havoc with local ferry schedules as well.

Cleopatra forces Marc Antony to kiss her asp.

And through all of this, speaking of driving men crazy, let us turn our attention once more to Cleopatra, a woman so manipulative, so ruthless, that she eventually had Marc Antony kissing her asp. All right.

By the Middle Ages, a time so named because almost all the men were between forty and sixty years old, women practically dominated the globe. Queen Elizabeth, Queen Isabella, and Nancy Reagan all had hundreds of servants and men-in-waiting at their beck and call.

With one stroke of the pen, they could declare war, imprison thousands, and reduce prices on carpets by as much as 15%. These were powerful, influential women, whose decrees and dictates could not be questioned, even by Geraldo Rivera.

Which brings us to the Renaissance, where Rubenesque women were seen everywhere, mostly because they were so large. In fact, many of these women carried enough poundage to be rewarded with their own zip codes, and it was not uncommon to see hordes of men erecting moats around them.

Also, around that time,* came Joan of Arc, a popular singer whose big hit, "Smoke Gets in Your Eyes," helped catapult her to one of the most powerful positions in France. And speaking of powerful French women, what about Josephine, who not only showed Napoleon how to conquer Spain, Germany, and England, but also how to dust behind his ears.

BY THE TWENTIETH CENTURY WOMEN DOMINATE THE GLOBE

That is, except for a few Islamic countries, where men can still have members of their harem burned at the stake, beheaded, or even slowly tortured to death by Bobby Vinton records.

Shere Shi'ite† (author of *The Shi'ite Report*) recommends broad economic sanctions against these countries but fails to address the larger issue: What if these same Arab states, in retaliation, decide to cut off our country's vital supply of high-grade halvah?

In this book, we will look at all the reasons that men hate themselves. We will offer charts, facts, figures, and thoroughly fabricated case studies. But beyond all that, we will document the women who hate these men as well. (And for reasons the men could have never imagined all by themselves!)

Indeed, to protect the integrity of this book's conclusions, and to justify the big advance we got, we've conducted our own in-depth survey and found out some pretty interesting facts. For instance, of the women we queried, only 93 million confessed to actually loving men, but of course their testimony had to be totally discarded—for the sake of accuracy.

---

*Give or take 300 years.
†Not to be confused with Cheri Hate, even though they're the same person. See Chapter 14.

Through the following chapters, we shall detail all the signs that positively identify a man who hates himself; the neglect he shows his wife, his children, and especially his sideburns are all dead giveaways. We will show what men who hate themselves eat, what they wear, and how they style their hair. Moreover, we will give specific physical descriptions of them, height, weight, and if they have any, depth.

And as if all this weren't hateful enough, we will also interview the women who make it a point to hate these men. We will delve into who these women are, where they came from, and how we can get them to go back. On top of that, *Men Who Hate Themselves* will offer men across the country a ten-point recovery program and, after that, a ten-point reupholstery program.

One last thing: Before we proceed, there may be those of you who assume that the author, for whatever reason, is acting out of a peculiar form of misogyny. Well, let us assure you, nothing could be further from the truth, as you will find that he's quite happily married and has a wife and child in Connecticut, a wife and child in North Carolina, and a wife and child in Tibet.

CHAPTER 2

LOVE, MARRIAGE, AND PREMARITAL DIVORCE

Much of the information in this chapter comes from a detailed questionnaire that we mailed across the country to men and women of either sex. And the results were quite intriguing. Actually, the results could have been even *more* intriguing, had we remembered to put on a return address. But that's neither here nor there.

One of the leading reasons that we found out that so many men hate themselves is because of their complex sexuality, and boy did we hear about some complexes! 12% of the male respondents admitted that they could only achieve an erection when sexually propositioned by a woman scantily dressed in black olives, but, of course, most of these guys were Greek.

And we uncovered facts even more surprising. For example, almost all the men we spoke to felt strongly pressured, after dining alone, to go home with themselves.

Of the women, only 14% of those who responded were female, but they quickly pointed out the reasons they hate men as well. Fully 56% of the women queried hated men who found it difficult to maintain an erection and an apartment in New York City at the same time.

However, of these women, 67% admitted to the fact that they were over eighty years old and still used a diaphragm, but only when they lied about their age.

WE ASKED SOME VERY PERSONAL QUESTIONS

1. Do you ever achieve orgasm through manual stimulation and, if there were no Manual around, would you consider a Carlos or a Raul?
2. Have you ever had sexual feelings toward your brother? Sister? Your podiatrist?
3. Do you believe in "Open Marriage," and if so, how late do you stay open?
4. Have you ever been a celibate? A halibut?
5. Who usually breaks up the involvement first? You? Your lover? Or the police?
6. When you fall asleep do you review the day's events in your mind? Or do you let Siskel and Ebert do it?
7. In order to stop you from "clinging," has your lover ever used Static Guard?
8. Have you ever used a dildo to reach orgasm? A dill pickle?
9. While making love, do you prefer touching your partner with tenderness? Or with gloves?
10. Do you engage in long and protracted foreplay? Fiveplay? Sixplay?
11. To arouse the person you're with would you lick them slowly at bedtime? Or quickly at Parcheesi?
12. Right now, do you have a regular lover? Have they ever been constipated?

This chapter is entirely based on the responses we received to these questions, from places as far away and as alien to the human mind as Nebraska. But sophisticated though we thought we were, the survey uncovered forms of sexuality heretofore unknown to us. For example, this response from Beverly Hills:

Didn't Like "Conventional" Sex

"The woman I lived with for over eleven years couldn't achieve orgasm in the conventional way, so she stopped going to conventions. But that wasn't the most disturbing part of the relationship.

"What really ticked me off was that she found shopping more of a sexual release than any she could have with me. As a matter of fact, on Rodeo Drive, particularly during half-price sales, she would many times achieve a full and satisfying 'storegasm.'

"Suffice to say, after returning home, this often resulted in her being unable to have sexual relations with me because—she claimed—that she was totally spent. This went on and on until finally, after much agonizing, I decided that I could no longer live with a woman who was 'buy-sexual.' "

And we received this response from a man who preferred that we didn't use his name, but identified himself as a recent Democratic candidate for the presidency of the United States.

Forced to Dress Up

"My wife would only get excited when I dressed up a certain way, preferably to resemble the governor of New York State. Even then, the only way to make sure she really got excited was for me to stand by the bed and recite the keynote address to the 1984 Democratic convention. Sometimes I had to do this two or three times. It gradually began to dawn on me, and this wasn't easy to accept, that I had married a latent 'Comosexual.' "

"Buy-Sexual"

THE MYTH OF THE MALE ORGASM

Obviously, this was a man who had minimal confidence and esteem. So little, we later found out, that he was obliged to fake orgasm, and this was just during masturbation.

Time and time again, as seasoned and professional as we thought we were, we were shocked by the revelations we heard. There were moments we wanted to flee from the room, scream, cry, but only when the movie channel was showing a Sylvester Stallone flick.

GENTLEMEN, GENETICS, AND GENITALS

Our research got into other interesting areas as well. We discovered there was an interesting correlation between how much a man hated himself and the size of his genitals.

For instance, a carpenter from Topeka, Kansas, was so well-endowed that he was given fifteen years in prison for raping a stewardess on an American Airlines flight, even though she was 28,000 feet above him at the time.

Another man, an employee of the telephone company, had such a small organ that he received a special grant from M.I.T. to participate in a study that sought to prove the existence of imaginary points. Subsequently, that study was successful, but only after six months of research that led to the discovery of his penis through an electron microscope.

To present our findings more thoroughly, the following chart represents the evidence that we uncovered. Let's see. Altogether we uncovered 439 men sleeping under wool blankets, 972 men wrapped in horse blankets, and 26,801 men hiding beneath various security blankets.

For the sake of accuracy we made every effort to accumulate these figures as quickly as possible, since, in the act of uncovering, the cold air was likely to diminish our measurements. This became pitifully obvious four hundred miles north of Juneau, when we removed the blubber comforter of an Eskimo. Unfortunately, the poor soul not only lost his erection, but his penis had to be immediately defrosted for twenty minutes inside a microwave.

MEN WHO HATE THEMSELVES: BY SIZE OF PENIS

¼″ or less	100 + %
1¹⁄₁₆″	99.4%
2¾″	92.8%
3¼″	82.1%
3½″	81.9%
4⁵⁄₃₂″	74.2%
5″	60.3%
6″	50%
7¹⁄₁₀₀″	5.1%
8¼″	1.7%
9⁵⁷⁄₉₃″	1.0%
Over 10″	.0000000003%
Over 15″	No data available*

*Researcher still in state of shock.

Finally, of all these men, 4% were fixated on their own penis, 3% were fixated on someone else's penis, and 93% were fixated on a hockey game. But clearly the most unexpected finding of all was that 99.7% of these men were also schizophrenic and allegedly reported that, during masturbation, they experienced simultaneous orgasm.

Most women, though, were clearly uninterested in the process of male maturbation, unless they had a headache that night. What concerned the majority of them was the tenderness and understanding that a man brought to the most intimate act known to human beings and his willingness, after climax, to take out the garbage.

Without a doubt, women from every economic and geographical sphere agreed that men were almost completely ignorant about how to excite them in the ways they most wanted, whether it was orally, manually, or most important of all, financially.

The following case study is a common example of what we heard.

Doug, Doris, and Her Clitoris

"During the first ten years of our marriage, Doug had a hard time finding my clitoris. First he looked under the bed, then under the pillow, and once he even dug up part of the front yard. Finally, I overcame my embarrassment and told him exactly where to look. You should have seen the shock on his face!"

High up on women's complaint lists were men's preference of sexual positions which, from their point of view, were really sexual impositions. Because of cultural role models and deep feelings of insecurity, we discovered, most men preferred to be on top—on top of the dresser, the refrigerator, anywhere but in bed.

Most men prefer being on top—of the dresser!

However, one of the primary driving forces behind women's anxiety was the feeling that time was running out to find Mr. Right. Nanette DiComo of Boulder, Colorado, was so distraught over this that it took more than twelve years for her therapist to finally convince her that her biological clock was really on Eastern Standard time, meaning that she had an extra hour to meet a man.

Unfortunately, Nanette, who was also quite petite, had a habit of meeting men who were absolutely wrong for her. She recounts a blind date with Ernie Vanderschmeer, the world-famous mosquito trainer.

An *Immense* Sexual Appetite

"Ernie had an immense sexual appetite. Well, actually, he had a sexual appetite for women who were immense. He shunned any female who tipped the scales at less than four hundred pounds and indeed preferred women who could not only tip the scales, but most of Manhattan as well.

"He was fond of coming over to his lady friends' homes, picking them up with a crane, and then chauffeuring

Ernie's wife got so fat that it broke his heart,
liver, kidneys . . .

them around town. We went out only once, but I heard his last affair ended tragically when the woman he eventually married broke his heart, by sitting on his chest."

MOST MEN AREN'T SUITABLE

Again and again, we heard of women finding out that the men they were going out with just weren't suitable; in fact, some of them weren't even capable of putting on sportsjackets. "It's hell," says Michaela Jackson, of Savannah, Georgia. "All the men I meet are into short-term relationships. How do I know? Because most of them are on Death Row."

It's the kind of situation Samantha Bupkes is quite familiar with. Beautiful and gifted, with degrees in electrical engineering and optometry, Samantha won a Nobel Prize for discovering the secret of curing glaucoma in electric eyes. Yet as attractive and talented as she is, even Samantha has remarkable trouble in finding a man who is truly on her level.

Stan, Dan, and the Tobacco Lobby

"You know, Stan didn't exactly have the greatest grasp of contemporary issues. He heard Dan Rather talking about the tobacco lobby and thought it was a place where you go to smoke.

"Also, his last girlfriend, Sheila, now I wouldn't exactly say that she was promiscuous but, in her high school sex education class, she was voted The Most Likely to Conceive.

"Oh Danny, Danny, you know I really lowered my standards to date him, since he was about 2′5″ tall."

THE TRUTH ABOUT THE MAN SHORTAGE

Samantha's relationship brings to light another critical issue, the man shortage, primarily caused by the glut of men who are short. Short men are everywhere you turn, but you can never see them, unless you're also searching the sidewalks for some spare change.

Naomi Mendez, of Peoria, only found her fiancé after accidentally stepping on him. Janet Fishbein rescued the man she lives with from drowning through the use of her quick wits and resolve, not to mention her dexterity with a bathroom plunger. Finally, there's Maxine Putro of Baltimore, who came home one summer's day only to discover that her husband Bernie had run off that afternoon and had eloped—with a gerbil!

The Man Shortage

However, let's not assume that it's merely short men who hate themselves. Tall men are every bit as prone to hating themselves as well. (Here, we define tall as any man who can peer down and see Wilt Chamberlain's bald spot.)

Wilbur Butte, of Shaker Heights, requires a tractor just to drag his mittens along. Ollie South, of North Plainfield, New Jersey, can't even limbo under a football goal post. And Jed Dubonk, from Montreal, was recently hired by NASA to retrieve defective satellites—with his hand.

Clearly, it's easy to see why these men feel they stand out in a crowd. And that's why, in most social situations, they feel the awkward need to crouch down—particularly when talking to God. On the plus side, tall men are usually taken more seriously than short men; even more so when they're threatening to destroy your condo with their big toe.

MINNIE'S AUTO-EROTIC DISCOVERY

Last, we come to the case study of Minnie Lazarus of Heckville, Minnesota, who found out a dark secret about her husband, Charlie, a renowned chicken mortician and inventor of Crocodile Tears, a soothing solution for alligators whose contacts occasionally dry out. This is how she describes it:

"Charlie is a wonderful provider, a loving husband, and father of our three beautiful children. Little did I suspect, after over twenty years of marriage, what a sick, tormented individual I had shared most of my life with.

"It started with small things, the smell of perfume in the car, a nylon stocking hidden in the glove compartment, and the queerest thing of all, lipstick on a speeding ticket. I suppose the normal reaction would have been anger, feelings of betrayal and inadequacy, all of that.

"But I wasn't going to let another woman win the man I put through law school without a fight. So one night, when he said he had to meet a client, I followed him in the station wagon. Well, let me tell you, it wasn't long before I saw her getting into Charlie's car.

"Blonde, beautiful, statuesque, she was so smug, so beautiful, so confident of herself, I felt like screaming. But I didn't have time. Suddenly, without warning, his car picked up speed. On either side of it I could make out teenage punks in their hot rods racing down the street—racing against my Charlie.

"The three cars were going over a hundred miles an hour down by the railroad tracks. It was all I could do to keep up and then, all at once, I heard a terrible crash. It was Charlie and he had sideswiped a garbage truck. One look and I knew that the car was totaled. It was a terrible sight.

"At that moment, I forgot about my anger and jealousy. I only wanted my Charlie to be all right, to talk to me. As I dashed out of my car, I stumbled over a high-heeled shoe, a shoulder pad, and a woman's pocketbook. I didn't care anymore as I ran to my Charlie.

"There he was, sprawled in the gutter, his skirt up over his head, his lipstick smeared, the wig hanging off his—uh, wig? Lipstick? Now wait a minute, I said to myself, something's definitely wrong here.

"Charlie buried his face in my lap and cried, smearing his mascara all over my blouse. Then it all came out. The man whom I had shared my bed with, whom I had loved and sacrificed for, this very same man was nothing less than—are you ready for this—the local *drag queen*. Believe me, it almost made me miss Bingo that night."

In the next chapter, we'll study many of the early life experiences, like Charlie's, that men have while growing up in their parents' homes. These are also known as the deformative years.

MEN WHO HATE THEMSELVES:
BY FAVORITE ROCK GROUP

The Beatles	01%
The Rolling Stones	01.1%
The Rolling Papers	01.11%
Black Sabbath	99%
White Sabbath	98.9%
Beige Sabbath	97%
The Jimi Hendrix Experience	50%
The Jimmy Carter Experience	500%
The Four Seasons	04%
The Four Tops	04%
The Four Skins	89%
The Jackson Five	17%
The Jesse Jackson Five	17.7%
The Police	28%
The Cops	28%
Huey Lewis and the News	09%
Jerry Lewis and the News	90%
Crosby, Stills, Nash & Young	41%
Bernstein, Schwartz, Gold & Katz	239%

Cy attributes the stormy relationship between his parents to his feeling that all relationships, in the end, eventually become suffocating, particularly if your lover is holding a pillow.

WILBUR KAPUTNIK'S PATERNAL PROBLEMS

Of course, there have been some men who have been even more directly persecuted by their fathers. Wilbur Kaputnik, a distributer of hole foods, such as doughnuts, bagels, and Life Savers, recounts his father's stern treatment of him:

"My father used to deliver threats, ultimatums, and yes, even pizza, he was that kind of guy. An exceptionally cold and brutal man, he used to take me out behind the woodshed every day and beat me, usually at poker, but occasionally at gin rummy as well.

"As you can see, he was a very disturbed person. I remember how he would force me to make my bed and then, after I did that, he would force me to make dressers, drawers, and once even a vanity table. He hated everyone. And things didn't improve any when my mother ran off with a professional sword swallower.

"When I look back, I feel sorry for him. He was a bitter, isolated man, whose only joy in life seemed to come from listening to an obscure piece of classical Chinese music entitled 'The Nutcracker Sweet and Sour.' "

Apparently one of the things that Wilbur was most ashamed of was his father's occupation, and this turned out to be a very common thread among Men Who Hate Themselves. By carrying out exhaustive research that lasted through most of our sushi platter, we were able to isolate those paternal careers that produced these feelings of self-loathing, we think.

CHAPTER 3

EARLY ADOLESCENCE (THE DEFORMATIVE YEARS): AGES 6–81

Protracted adolescence is quite a common occurrence among many men, and there are numerous reports of those well into their seventies who report their first pubic hair. Cy Napse, a whiz kid at 105, still enjoys dipping little girls' pigtails into inkwells. But just because Cy has the maturity of a nine-year-old child, don't assume that this has hampered him in the business world.

Actually, after school, he's a major financier whose skills at mergers produced The Washington Post Cereal Company, an outfit that enjoyed considerable success the moment it started marketing a new type of Shredded Wheat, one in the shape of Colonel Oliver North.

Yet despite his material success, Cy recalls an early childhood incident that brings tears to his eyes. Either that, or he has an allergy.

"Once, after my mother brought me home from school, I remember my father screaming at her at the top of his lungs, 'I can't stand it anymore! You have the face of an eighty-year-old woman!' Yes, I remember the entire incident quite clearly, even though I was only sixty-five at the time."

MEN WHO HATE THEMSELVES: BY FATHER'S OCCUPATION	
Anchovy trainers	23%
Volunteer arsonists	39%
Anvil salesmen	51%
Water bedouins	7%
Loincloth repairmen	32%
Piano movers and shakers	44%
Stuffed dermatologists	88%
Bushmen (appointees of George Bush)	371%

As this chart clearly indicates, early parental influences affect both men in the prime of their life, as well as men in the prime of their senility. Quite often, mothers and fathers don't mean to be cruel, but try explaining this to Phil Bopski, of Palo Alto, California, who remains bitter to this day because his parents put powdered milk in his baby bottle.

Or to Regis Grillox, of Houston, who remembers the day his parents bronzed his baby shoes—while he was still wearing them. Even today, Regis struggles to come to terms with his emotions, but while he's made them a good-faith offer, it still looks like he'll be forced to arbitrate.

All in all, for a period of over five years, we collected data. We received thousands upon thousands of letters and this one is a fairly typical example of those we threw away.

HIS FATHER BURNT HIS BRIDGES BEHIND HIM

"When I was growing up, my parents moved around a lot, but they never left me a forwarding address. It's not surprising. My father was the type of man who burnt his bridges behind him, his caps, and he once even tried setting fire to his root canal work.

"Still, I know that I really loved him. The man was sixty-five years old and had the incredible body of a twenty-year-old swimmer, though he never seemed quite capable of locating the head.

"I remember the day we moved to Milwaukee. That was the city where they sent me to this private school. What a place! The nuns would give me incredible beatings every day, which was kind of strange, since I was attending yeshiva.

"Yet, when I look back, I realize a lot of things that I didn't appreciate before. Sure, my parents could've spoiled me, but that would have first entailed taking me out of the refrigerator."

Probing the male psyche deeper and deeper, a number of things became plainly obvious. All too often there was unfinished business between men and their parents; and, no matter how hard their offspring tried to reason with them, most parents refused to put all their worldly assets in their son's names. Jordan Rivers, of Kalamazoo, shows us that a wealthy upbringing can be just as damaging as a poor one.

GREW UP IN AFFLUENT NEIGHBORHOOD

"The neighborhood where I was brought up was so affluent that we fought our gang wars with mercenaries. Dad had a rigid personality, to the point that mom often used him as an ironing board.

"It was a strange childhood. You see, my father never got over the fact that in 1911 my grandmother went down on the *Titanic*, but, as we later found out, it was on the whole crew.

"Instead he preferred to trace our family history back to the days of the American Revolution when our ancestors proudly instigated the Boston Herbal Tea Party, successfully turning the entire harbor and parts of Martha's Vineyard the color of Red Zinger.

"It's true. With my father, just the thought of Christmas and family was enough to warm the cockles of his heart, but if that didn't work, we made sure to put a hot plate across his chest."

ELAYNE AND RUTH TELL DUDLEY THE TRUTH

Besides parents, siblings, especially sisters, can have a significant effect on how little a man thinks of himself. Dudley Schmendrake, of Wichita Falls, recalls that his older sister Ruth was pre-med, his younger sister Elayne pre-law, while they considered him pre-fetus.

"You could register their hostility toward me on a seismograph," he asserts indignantly. And when you examine the record there's absolutely no doubt that Dudley's speaking the truth, quite a rare thing for a man, since it occurs about as frequently as an ice age.

According to his recollections, Dudley's sister Ruth used to play cruel tricks on him. She once told him that when he was born there was incredible confusion, with the doctors spending most of the afternoon and much of the evening slapping each other. The story instantly made Dudley burst into tears—on his 35th birthday too!

A miserable woman, by all accounts, sister Ruth was a compulsive eater who was to mysteriously disappear in Europe during suction lipectomy. From then on, for years afterward, the only trace of her was a faint voice emanating from the tip of a straw.

However, sister Elayne was a much different story. An

obsessive personality, she always insisted on watering the plants before leaving the house, even though they were all artificial.

A mere fifty-five years younger than Dudley, he still recalls her quite vividly. "I can even remember her favorite book," he says with a grin on his face. *"The Jogging Shoes of the Fisherman.* It was about the winner of the Boston marathon who, through a strange twist of fate, becomes Pope and excommunicates anyone caught without Reeboks, even if they're not Catholic."

To this day, Dudley truly believes that Elayne was secretly enamored of him. Well, upon further study into his childhood, we think that perhaps *enameled* is a better word, since she was always cementing little tiles all over his body.

THE UNCONSCIOUS MESSAGES MEN RECEIVE FROM THEIR MOTHERS (USUALLY ON THEIR ANSWERING MACHINES)

"I'm sick and tired of talking to a machine. Aren't you ever home? Where are you? Out all night with some floozy! Just like your father! When I was the one who worked all day and all night to put you through—(BEEP) I hate that beep! Do you know how much this call is costing me? A lot you care they're forcing me to share my oxygen tent with a family of kangaroos. I hate Australia! Why you sent me here I'll never—(BEEP) That beep is driving me crazy! Is that your plan? To drive me crazy? So that you can inherit the Kaiser's invasion plans? Never! I'll take them to my grave with—(BEEP) Why aren't you there? Wasn't I always there for you? That's right. Who put up your bail when you were convicted of playing canasta with an underage panda? Me, that's who. But do you—(BEEP) Tell me, is playing the spoons a living? At least you could try playing the knives and forks as well. Oh I don't know—(BEEP) I remember when you used to come home from embalming school, the smell of Aqua Velva on your breath, and I was so proud of you. Such a—(BEEP) Good boy. Such a nice boy. Such a—(BEEP) —Such—(BEEP) Su—(BEEP BEEP BEEP) Listen I know you're—(BEEP)"

THE UNCONSCIOUS MESSAGES MEN RECEIVE FROM THEIR FATHERS (USUALLY ON THEIR ANSWERING MACHINES)

"Hey, can I spend a few days over there? Your mother is driving me crazy!"

The above profile is a classic case of a parental relationship which is referred to, in professional circles, as "Mother Superior/Father Inferior." Men Who Hate Themselves are frequently the product of this kind of troubled union.

A clear example of this is Herbert Schismo, of Fort Worth, who recalls that every night in front of the family his mother would repeatedly strike his father, often carrying a picket sign until her demands were met.

Yet even before she married his father, it was clear that she had a negative view of the opposite sex. "Most of the men I've met are a dime a dozen, which is highway robbery, even taking into account the rate of inflation." An angry, frustrated woman, why she married his father remains a mystery to this day, since he was an alcoholic musician capable of playing only in one key—Whiskey!

Once, Herbert tried to broach the subject of his father with his mother. He pleaded with her to be more tolerant by arguing that alcoholism was just a disease. "Oh yeah," she retorted. "Think I was born yesterday. Next thing you'll try and tell me is that cancer is just a disease too."

Obviously, she was a difficult woman. And due to her influence, Herbert has always felt compelled to impress his dates by making sure he takes them to the highest-priced restaurants in town. Places so expensive that it was usually required, right on the menu, to make a down payment on the house salad.

HERBERT TALKS ABOUT HIS HORRIBLE LOSS

Today, the memory of his mother and father still haunts Herbert. But there's one moment, in particular, that he'll never forget:

"Look, this is not easy to talk about. I experienced a horrible loss the day both my parents died in that car crash. Yes, I remember it quite clearly. Because I had bet on the Yankees to win."

The next chapter picks up on this important theme. [P]roviding we can figure out, by then, exactly what that theme was.

MEN WHO HATE THEMSELVES: BY COUNTRY	
France	01.1%
India	04.3%
Zimbabwe	28.5%
Yugoslavia	47.2%
Italy	00.0%*
Canada	50.2%
Thailand	02.8%
Germany	93.4%
England	93.5%
Tahiti	00.7%
Brazil	02.9%
Brooklyn	87.6%
Denmark	14.7%
Japan	00.1%
Syria	06.7%
Israel	07.6%
United States	105.9%

*Actually, the figure was even less.

CHAPTER 4

MEN WHO SHOULD HATE THEMSELVES, BUT DON'T

Men of any age or economic group, and this is not widely known, can also suffer from PMS (Premarital Syndrome), which usually strikes before asking any woman for a second date. So before calling again they wait a little while, customarily five or six years, in the hope that the woman will go seek another lover, preferably one in Bangladesh.

Now, while there's every reason for these men to hate themselves, most of them don't, although they might occasionally chastise themselves by nicking their faces with a razor. But no matter what they do, the effect that men afflicted with PMS can have on women is all too often devastating. Take the case of Abigail who . . .

Cried Herself a River

"After my last boyfriend left me, I stayed in bed for a month and cried myself a river, although, since I lived in Boston, the river was soon polluted and I was eventually fined over two million dollars by the EPA."

MISOGYNY AND MAURICE CHEVALIER

Yes, misogyny expresses itself in many ways, but rarely in the music of Maurice Chevalier. Quite often it's displayed by the lack of concern men seem to have for the women they're with. It happened to Gloria Estabar, of San Salvador, when she broke off her engagement to a Nicaraguan rebel, after he refused to use a Contra-ceptive. Here's another example of how men vent their rage.

"Mark was very good at expressing his anger, but it never did me any good, since he usually expressed it in fluent Latvian. I will admit this, though, he did have a talent for getting things off his chest, especially the bureau I once put on it.

"Day after day, he would throw one tantrum after another and, when he ran out of tantrums, he would throw TV sets, toasters, I mean the guy really terrified me. Especially when he did his Shelley Winters imitations. I don't know.

"Things deteriorated quickly and he started calling me lots of names—stupid, incompetent, and once even Seymour Mendez, though I never found out why. I guess the last straw was the night we went to a very expensive French restaurant where he insisted on splitting the check—with an ax!"

WHY TONY WAS FULL OF BALONEY

Another category of man who should hate himself is the vain, self-centered type, like Tony. Sharon first met him on the set of a Hollywood film where she had a job as the director's chair. Tony at the time was starring in a new sci-fi

Splitting the check

movie in which a tiny little Mexican—wearing a sombrero—
explodes out of his chest. The film was called *Illegal Alien*.

"Tony was this incredibly sexy guy. In fact, this wom-
en's magazine came to him and wanted him to be their
centerfold, although he later declined when he found out
where the staple would go. But despite the fact that he
was strong and virile, he was also withholding. So much
so, I thought that I was entitled to a refund.

"Listen, I tried to improve the situation. One night I
placed a copy of the Comma-Sutra (that ancient sex manual for high school English teachers) on his pillow, but he
became completely impotent. It then took me three weeks

to explain to him that *syntax* was not a special charge the government put on oral sex.

"Yeah, looking back, I suppose the guy was really only concerned with himself. We'd make love and he'd turn to me and say, 'It was good for me. Was it good for I?'

"All in all, when you think about it, Tony was pretty self-centered. After we broke up, my friends told me that he went to see a doctor who only treated people with incredible egos. An 'I' doctor, I guess."

Soon after this relationship, Sharon underwent a complete change. She became a spiritual being and—in six months—did est, turned into a Hare Krishna, and then married and divorced the Maharishi. Suffice to say, for tax purposes, she's now computing a Prophet-and-Loss statement.

SO, DO MEN HAVE ANY GOOD POINTS?

A substantial majority of the women we spoke to felt that you could count all of men's good points on the fingers of one of Venus de Milo's hands. Time after time, they cited instances of incredible cruelty, abuse, with some of them being subjected, by force, to some of the most heinous colognes ever conceived.

These revelations were shocking and tragic. Cynthia Hymen, of Pittsburgh, reported that her husband tied her to the couch and then forced her to watch a porno film about a family of Eskimos and a small walrus, called *Nanookey of the North*. Deborah Blanchard, a stenographer, told us that her boyfriend Ken was so unsavory that a co-op board had recently turned down his application for a one-bedroom apartment—in Beirut!

But of all the women we spoke to, one poor soul stands out in particular. For there was no doubt that she lived in mortal fear of her husband, a maniac named Fred Turner, whose mission in life was to decolorize all films made in the past forty years and turn them black and white. Here is her story.

CONFESSIONS OF A BATTERED WIFE

"I tried hiding it from my children, my neighbors, even my mother and father, but soon everyone was beginning to notice that I was a battered wife. As I recall, the situation was getting so bad that my husband was battering me two, maybe three times a day, forcing me to sit in a large mixing bowl while he added eggs, milk, and some flour.

"It was humiliating. The way he called me his little Flapjack. But what was I to do? I depended on him for emotional, financial, and yes, even arch support. That Fred! I'm so furious at him! He's waffled on every promise he's ever made to me.

"Oh yes, in the beginning, we were the French Toast of

Battered wife

the town. But little did I realize what he meant when he said that he preferred to see me in pancake makeup.

"Luckily, the police caught him one night as he was chasing me down the street—with an eggbeater. It was the turning point in his life. Fred went into therapy and learned to redirect his hostilities, thank God. Now he just batters shrimp."

VINCENT—THE ART COLLECTOR

Of course, in the real world, a man who should hate himself is often not that easy to spot. Vincent was such a man. An avid art collector, he had Art Deco hung in his living room, Art Nouveau hung in his dining room, and Art Carney hung in the bathroom. Yet this, in and of itself, was no great insight into the type of man he really was. However, to the trained eye, there were some clues as to his actual perverse state of mind.

Most revealing of these was the choice of aquatic creatures he kept in his private study. In one large tank, he had piranhas from the Amazon, and in another one, from Israel, he had an amazing collection of fighting gefilte fish. They were frightening little demons that would fight voraciously over matzoh balls, chicken livers, and, in particular, small slivers of rabbis.

A man of untold wealth ($2.47, to be exact, so you see why he didn't like to talk about it), Vincent would go to any length to indulge his numerous pleasures. But where did he get his money? Rumors persisted he had made a killing in the market, but later it turned out that he had merely sacrificed a chicken outside a local 7-11! What everybody seemed to have forgotten is that Vincent was a solitary man, impervious to innuendo, who lived quietly by the sea, alone, in a small cardboard cottage.

Sylvia Enters the Picture

It was a situation that would have continued unchanged except for Sylvia. She was an exceptional woman in every respect who, despite her poor beginnings, continued to live in poverty. A volunteer at a local welfare clinic, she aided low-income people in their constant struggle against drugs, crime, and the morbid obsession they were Ricky Ricardo.

It was there one morning where she met Vincent. For he was also a powerful idealist. A staunch defender not only of the homeless but of the co-opless and condoless as well. Suffice to say, Sylvia found herself instantly smitten. Infatuated by Vincent's quiet charm, his dignity, plus his delightful habit of yodeling just before brunch.

Soon she was his constant companion, and soon after that, his wife. She quickly discovered all the wonderful little things that only a wife can. For instance, Vincent truly enjoyed pampering himself on the weekends and, by the time Monday rolled around, it was all she could do to pull those diapers off him.

However, beneath their storybook romance lurked a deep, dark secret. A morbid series of events that started to unfold with a knock on the door, early one Sunday morning.

Sylvia Learns Vincent's Terrible Secret

"Believe me, the day that the police came and started digging up our backyard, I had no idea of what was going on—no idea of how sick the man I married really was. I remember the inspector in charge of the whole operation was a tough guy, but even he was trembling at the sight of all those dismembered, rotted forms that the police were unearthing.

"One after another, they brought them up from the ground, some had been stabbed, others shot-gunned, there must have been over thirty of them, boxes of Corn Flakes,

Cereal murderer

Shredded Wheat, Quaker Oats, you name it. Lord, how could I face the world again knowing that I, Sylvia Kellogg, had married a cereal murderer!"

It took a lot of therapy and hard work for Sylvia to recover from this traumatic experience but today, we're pleased to report, Sylvia has remarried. This time to a gifted young painter, a Post-Impressionist, who does remarkable canvases depicting the inner life of Post Raisin Bran, Post Grape-Nuts, etc.

A WOMAN SHOULD STAND BEHIND HER MAN

Let's face it. A lot of times Men Who Should Hate Themselves require that extra little push, be it off a bridge—or a balcony, to realize how loathsome they really are.

Yet many times a bridge, balcony, or even a conveniently open window on a 747 are just not available and, if they are, there are often long waiting lines before you get your chance. But what about the busy woman who refuses to take a number, who doesn't have the time to just stand around all day while waiting to push some guy off a cliff?

Well, we think you'll be inspired by the story of Georgia.

Under a Lot of Pressure

"My Gil is under a lot of pressure, about sixty thousand fathoms, if my estimates are correct. I remember the exact moment he went overboard. There was only a split second to act when he screamed out, 'Life Saver! Life Saver!!' So I did, throwing him a Wintergreen, his favorite flavor.

"But we weren't always at odds. On the whole, he was a rather attractive sort and—I guess I have to admit this—I was easily hooked. Yet, for some reason, it was only after he took me out of the net and weighed me that he proposed.

"The first few years were a period of adjustment. However I gradually realized that Gil was definitely out of my league. For one thing, I attended a School of Nursing and he, at the same time, attended a School of Guppies. There were other things as well.

"For even at the most rudimentary social functions he was like a fish out of water, always flapping around on the carpet, with the only thing that could calm him down a peanut-butter-and-jellyfish sandwich.

"It became too much. Like an octopus, the jerk was always all over me, and, even after dry-cleaning I could never get all that black ink off my blouse. Eventually, I came to the decision that I had to throw him back, and I tell you I'm not sorry for what I did. After all, he always did claim to be a man of incredible depth."

During a follow-up interview, we were able to get Gil to tell us exactly what his feelings were by baiting him with a few questions. He confessed that life under the Pacific was hard, especially in trying to avoid man-eating sharks, but that he felt better prepared for it after the Reagan administration.
Currently, he's emotionally involved with a piano tuna.

HOW TO RECOGNIZE A MAN WHO DOESN'T HATE HIMSELF

- Shows affection for himself, even in public.
- Remembers his name in the morning.
- Talks to himself a great deal, and even listens to what he has to say.
- Not embarrassed to introduce himself to his parents.
- Never feels obligated to fake erection.

HOW TO RECOGNIZE A MAN WHO DOES HATE HIMSELF

- Obsession with death, dying, and going on singles' weekends.
- Loss of interest in sex, relationships, and the *David Letterman Show*.
- Tends to sleep more than ten years at a time.
- Feels that he's not getting older, only fatter.
- Has performance anxiety, even during masturbation.

CHAPTER 5

GROVELING, PLEADING, WHINING, BEGGING, PLUS OTHER POPULAR SEXUAL POSITIONS

"Most men give their wives multiple orgasms. Unfortunately, multiples of zero."

—CHERI HATE (author of *The Hate Report*)

Remember the days when a woman had to be a combination wife, mother, and doormat? Well, those days are long gone. Thanks to Women's Liberation, it's now the men who must conform to their wives' lifestyles, especially in the sexual area. Failure to adjust often means banishment to the couch, the basement, or in extreme cases, Milwaukee.

It's a fact. Men just aren't being afforded the respect they deserve. A former Iranian hostage told us of the ordeal he went through when a woman from the C.I.A. debriefed him, and he was left without underwear.

THOSE ONE-NIGHT STANDS

Wherever you go nowadays, all you hear are countless women complaining that all men seem to be interested in are one-night stands, particularly when their bedrooms are too small to lie down in. However, examine the issues more closely and you'll see the real problem is not that men are grinning and bearing it. The real problem is that so few women want to see it.

In our first case study, we look at the plight of a man who wishes to remain anonymous, but whose wishes we've ignored and who is really Emmanuel Bleckerman of 1911 Palo Alto Drive, San Bernardino, California, Apt. 3C.

Here he tells us of his harrowing home life.

PUNISHED HIM WITH SEX

"Marie used sex to punish me. And when she really got fed up, she punished me with her cooking, often forcing me to fall to my knees and prostrate myself before her meatloaf. It was ironic. Because at first I played the dominant male role, intimidating her not only sexually but often at marbles as well.

"However, as the months went by, I noticed a subtle change in her behavior. Perhaps it was all those Sensitivity Training courses she took with Yasir Arafat, or the way I would frequently catch her trying to reuse postage on letter bombs. You know what? I think the final humiliation came the night I reached for her in the dark and wound up kissing Simon Wiesenthal."

Because of fear, hostility, and the increasing suspicion that most men are not Robert Redford, women in astounding numbers are becoming turned off to sex. So much so that hapless men from coast to coast are going to any lengths just to excite them.

How He Eventually Aroused Her

"Believe me, I tried just about everything to stimulate my wife's clitoris. I first started trying to read it the works of Voltaire, next those of Edna St. Vincent Millay and even Chaucer. I tell you, after months and months of trying, the only hint of a response I got was when I started reading it sections of *Airport*.

More and more, we're seeing *Sexual Politics* become a campaign issue in the bedroom. But perhaps no more flagrantly than in the next case study, where we meet one woman who insists on what we may call "radical" forms of lovemaking. It's enough to make a true-blooded American see "red"!

OLGA, TROTSKY, AND GORBACHEV

"Olga was always jetting all over the place, to parties in Moscow, Leningrad, Havana, Peking, and East Berlin. On our very first date, I recall, she said that she was attracted to me because I had a beard like Trotsky, and a forehead like Gorbachev.

"However, despite her attraction to me, I soon realized that I would have no chance of sleeping with her unless I made a pledge to destroy the fabric of western civilization, especially if it were polyester.

"Well, maybe it was the Cuban cigars she smoked, or the way she jiggled that tattoo of Khruschev on her chest, I don't know. All I know is that maybe I wasn't cut out to be involved with a real socialist butterfly."

Unfortunately, men who become involved with this type of woman find out—all too soon—the true meaning of the word "Fidel" in fidelity. So, given this fact, it wasn't long before Olga was running around town with a Marxist plastic surgeon who specialized in bun tucks.

His advertising motto was "The Ends Justify The Means," but what he was particularly noted for was his practice of not using anesthesia. Instead, he would completely numb his patients by reciting long excerpts from *Das Kapital*.

Yet strangely enough, even though he was a dyed-in-the-wool Stalinist, what gave him more of a thrill than anything else in the world was good old-fashioned American base-ball. Indeed, when he went to a game, the only time you ever found him sitting down was during *The Star-Spangled Banner*.

Of course, men like this, those who derive some satisfaction from life, are the rare exception. A significant number of American men are finding that, no matter how unrewarding their relationships are, they still stand a better chance of being totally humiliated and abused if they journey to an exotic land.

RON SEEKS AN UNREWARDING RELATIONSHIP

Ronnie Osmond, a Mormon whose seven wives filed a history-making, class action divorce suit against him, decided to skip town and pursue his masochism south of the border.

Originally, he was hired to teach Spanish as a second language to Mexicans, but it took him six months just to get across the meaning of the word "español."

Well, that wasn't the Mexicans' fault, nor was it the San Andreas fault; it was his fault.

For Ronnie's skills as a teacher were severely limited by the fact that he was totally illiterate (a condition, by the way, which never proved to be a hindrance during the 42 years he served as an advertising account executive). Still, he confesses, he would have left Mexico if it weren't for Rita.

Tijuana Dance and Hold My Hand

"Yes, my delicious Rita, with her ruby-red lips, jet-black hair, and incredible olive skin, which unfortunately didn't come pitted. I can still remember the night I spotted her in a Tijuana cafe—well, to tell you the truth, spotted her fifty dollars during a floating crap game—but no, that didn't matter.

"For the magic of the evening had us completely caught up in its spell. I donned a sombrero and Rita told me that I had everything Cesar Romero had, minus looks and charm.

"Tequila, more and more tequila, the cumulative effects were soon affecting my judgment and all of a sudden I didn't know if I was coming or arriving. Was it Rita in my arms, Sophia Loren, or perhaps even Leonard Nimoy? I didn't know and I didn't care.

"I carried her to my room, the one over the cafe, and we made love with the TV on. As she expertly aroused me, using a bilingual approach, there was a late-night western playing that I'll never forget. The movie was *The James Gang,* starring James Earl Jones, James Earl Ray, James Earl Carter, James Earl of Kent and James Earl, as himself. But why even mention that?

"While Rita thrust up and down, looking to bring herself to climax, I could feel the walls of her vagina. They were soft, warm, perhaps in need of a little plastering. Faster and faster, the images blur, I was struggling to breathe, struggling to satisfy her animal desires.

"I guess all that excitement was what sent me into cardiac arrest, but you know what? The hospital refused to set bail. The corrupt bastards!"

But There's a Happy Ending

Yes, it's a grim tale, but not without a happy ending. For when she was last seen, Rita was in her favorite cafe valiantly helping a choking victim to expire. While Ronnie, several years later, would use these cheap and tawdry experiences south of the border as the basis for writing a long-running Broadway hit, *Morning Becomes Electralux,* a play, in the grand tradition of Eugene O'Neill, about a small family of Mexican vacuum cleaners.

Of course, we could have said that the show is really cleaning up at the box office, but that type of cheap remark is truly beneath us. (All right, just barely.)

Next we come to perhaps the most widespread form of groveling and pleading, albeit you may not recognize it in all its clever disguises, but it's revealed by the compulsion men demonstrate—in the presence of the opposite sex—to show they have a sense of humor. A forthcoming book, by Steven Klausner and a certain D.R., describes this common syndrome in agonizing detail. It's entitled:

PUNILINGUS (THE IRRESISTIBLE URGE TO COMMIT FOREPLAY ON WORDS)

In this deeply insightful work, published simultaneously in Borneo and Cambodia, the authors detail a number of things that men say to amuse women, often with humiliating results. Here are some remarks that have been overheard at various cocktail parties:

"That's strange. Your last boyfriend had a sexual emission every time he was in the presence of certain French cheeses. Well, I guess he suffered from Brie-ejaculation. Ha-ha-ha!! Not funny, huh?"

"So you were in Detroit and you couldn't find a tampon. Maybe you should have looked for a brand named *Motex*. Hey, where are you going? I was just kidding!"

"You don't say. Your first husband tried to do what to your cat? Really. I suppose you could call him one hell of a Purr-vert. Thanks. My sports jacket needed just a dash of red wine."

"It took a lot of courage to tell me that. Your father was a notorious voyeur who terrorized the washrooms of Chinese restaurants. Hmm. Guess you'd have to say the guy was a regular Peking Tom. Wait! Wait! Put that chair down!!"

Purr-vert

"So big deal. You were going out with this real estate agent who gave you what, a sexual disease. There's nothing to cry about. It was probably only Herpes Duplex. Uh, listen, is that gun loaded?"

"No kidding. Your brother could only be satisfied by twin Swedish cars? That's incredible. They must have been Vulvos. Get it! Sure, I'd love to come over and see your collection of flame throwers."

"Tell me what happened then. You came home and found him in the arms of Jerry Falwell? Well, what were they having, Moral Sex? O.K. O.K. I'm sorry, O.K."

EXERCISES MEN WHO HATE THEMSELVES HATE

Chin-ups	Sit-ups
Push-ups	Jogging
Aerobics	Weight lifting
Rowing	Bicycling
Swimming	Calisthenics

EXERCISES MEN WHO HATE THEMSELVES LOVE

Exercises in futility

CHAPTER 6

PROBING THE MALE LIE-BIDO

The male lie-bido is the part of the brain that is responsible for falsehood, pretension, chicanery, and résumé writing. Recent clinical evidence has clearly identified the male lie-bido as the source of all exaggeration and bravado, plus it's where the words "eight inches" most frequently emanate from.

From the first, our research was very extensive, and it produced some intriguing results. Fans of George Wallace, for example, appeared to be compelled to tell white lies. On the other hand, it seemed that many men had a habit of telling trumped-up stories, but these guys were easily detectable, particularly if they weren't Donald Trump.

What follows is the case study of a man whose pathological lie-bido became so malignant that it could only be removed during a six-hour operation, in Geneva, by a team of specialists employing the latest breakthroughs in polo mallets.

VOTED "MOST LIKELY TO DECEIVE"

"Back in high school, and I'll never forget this, I was voted 'The Most Likely To Deceive.' Would I kid you? Ha-ha-ha! But it was at the Columbia School of Journalism that I learned my most important lesson: Never let the facts obscure the truth.

"Believe me, that changed my life. You believe me? Ha-ha-ha-ha!! Wait, this is the best. I remember I once got sex off this one chick because I told her I only had six months to live. And the dumb broad bought it. Ha-ha-ha! The truth was I only had four months. Ha-ha-ha-ha!!!!!"

THE COMPOSITION OF THE MALE LIE-BIDO

Physically, the male lie-bido is composed of a lot of nerve cells, and you can be sure these cells have a lot of nerve. If a chart of a man's brain were superimposed over a map of Los Angeles, the male lie-bido would be found exactly at 2930 Sepulveda Boulevard, right next to "The Temple of Oral Love," or, for those of you not familiar with the city, about halfway between Paramount Studios and the offices of William Morris.

Indeed, astounding new research from the A.M.A. (American Macho Association) has shown the male lie-bido to be an intricate network of neurons, ganglia and blood vessels that, in x-ray photographs, seem to bear a striking resemblance to Richard Nixon.

But perhaps the best way to understand the intricate workings of the male lie-bido is as follows.

Common Utterances of the Male Lie-bido (to Women)

"I'll call you this week."

"I've never felt this way before."

"God, oh God, you're the best!"

"Why haven't I met anyone like you before?"

"Me married? Whatever gave you that idea?"

"When I'm with you, I forget about all the others."

"Me? Make a pass at your best friend? Honey, don't be ridiculous, she's not even in your class."

"I'm working late."

"I can't believe it. I never came this fast."

"Well, it's not a huge trust fund, but . . ."

"Of course, I have to admit, it was a low-budget film, but it did win first prize at the New Delhi Film Festival.

"Really, I could've sworn you were a model."

"Marriage is the only way, I feel, that two people can really be close to each other."

"You know, I thought about you every minute I was away."

"No, no, the reason I'm turning the lights off is because it's more romantic."

"I'm not dating anyone else."

"Why should I feel queasy about making love while you're having your period? It's a perfectly natural function."

"Two can live as cheaply as one."

"Honey, she must have mistaken me for someone else."

"O.K., tomorrow night, I'll cook."

"You're kidding! I thought that was your natural color."

"Listen, even the thought of a homosexual relationship disgusts me."

"This is your daughter? I thought you were sisters."

"Of course, even graduating sum cumma laude from Harvard can't open up all the doors."

"Wouldn't you know it. Last night my Mercedes blew an oil ring."

*"Uh, well, last night my, uh, Mercedes blew an
oil ring."*

"Really, I'm turned on by the smell."

"Your mother is a great lady."

"I'll do more than respect you in the morning, I'll admire
you."

"A condom? But the only person I've had sex with for the
past twenty years is my wife."

"So far, we've raised about fifteen or sixteen million, but
that's just start-up capital. Look, I must be boring you."

"I swear, these magazine subscription guys are really ob-
noxious. Imagine calling eleven o'clock at night."

"Honey, you don't have crow's feet."

"Don't you think I feel as bad as you do?"

"Did anyone ever tell you how cute you are when you're asleep?"

"I promise to love, cherish, and obey."

Common Utterances of the Male Lie-bido (To Other Men)

Naturally, the male lie-bido doesn't only operate with women. It's often activated at "male only" gatherings, such as card games, locker rooms, and top-level corporate strategy sessions conducted in adjoining urinals.

During these ritual gatherings, men feel obligated to expand upon the events of the previous evening, with some exaggeration of course. For example, the man who says, "She made my blood boil" may merely be referring to the fact that she simply stuck his face in the microwave. Here are some other common utterances.

"Yeah, I know I look tired. Must've been those sixteen-year-old twins."

"She must have come at least eight or nine times."

"Just like Sophia Loren, only bigger boobs."

"Sleep? Who got to sleep? Know what I mean, Charlie?"

"Hey, forget about it. She had my pants off the second I walked in."

". . . then she took the whole thing in her mouth while I . . ."

"Listen, I never paid for it in my whole life."

"Are you kidding, I saw parts of Sheila that her gynecologist never even dreamed of."

"Man, she was screaming so loud I thought I was gonna go deaf."

"So I said, 'Honey please, I have to go to work.'"

"She told me I was even better than Jack Kennedy."

"After I was through, she wanted to pay me."

MEN WHO HATE THEMSELVES: BY FAVORITE SEXUAL FANTASY	
Being Totally Dominated	13%
By Green Bay Packers	93%
Having Multiple Partners	06%
Of a Law Firm	54%
Animal Sex	50%
With an Understanding Pony	51%
With a Wild and Crazy Wildebeest	97%
Sex With Animal Crackers	52%
Getting Cruelly Whipped	45%
Inside a Blender	128%
Engaging in Group Sex	01%
With In-Laws	99%
Making Love on a Beach	.001%
An Iranian Beach	128%
Six Hours of Mutual Masturbation	72%
With a Mutual Fund Salesman	72.1%
Being Completely Tied Up	26%
By Irate Longshoremen	62%
Getting a Light Spanking	05%
From Shirley Temple	13%
From Arnold Schwarzenegger	129%

CHAPTER 7

IMPERSONAL ADS

Men and women searching for just the right person to loathe forever would be hard-pressed if it weren't for the efforts of a number of singles' publications created exclusively for them. One of the most successful of these is *New Dork* magazine, a bimonthly periodical that comes out once a year.

Editor-in-Chief Clint Westwood found the woman he recently murdered through just such an ad, and he's eager to share his surefire formula for pain and humiliation with others.

"But you have to be careful," cautions Westwood. "The man who advertises 'Zany, Live-Wire' may just be another one of those crazy electricians. What's more, someone who claims that he's a 'Spirited Man' could be a chronic imbiber of scotch, vodka, or even cleaning fluid. Finally, the guy seeking a 'New Lease on Life,' well, he's probably just been evicted."

Suffice to say, women aren't the only sex that can be led astray; so can men, and Westwood offers them advice as well. "Some women who advertise 'I'm Absolutely Gorgeous' may not be entirely misleading a man—assuming he's fond of crustaceans."

WHAT ABOUT THE "COVER GIRL" TYPE?

Likewise, the "Cover Girl Type" could be exactly that, providing the cover is the one of *National Geographic*. Yet don't dismiss this woman entirely. She may have a lot going for her. Normally, she's unpretentious, and possesses a great degree of native intelligence, however, of the kind more frequently associated with bushmen.

Also, be cautious of abbreviations. One unfortunate secretary from Des Moines learned only too late that SWM wasn't Straight White Male but, in reality, Sadistic Wichita Minstrel.

What follows is a compilation of "Strictly Impersonal" ads that were scheduled to run in the next issue of *New Dork* had the editor-in-chief not been forced, by the magazine's board of directors, into early strangulation.

I JUST IDOLIZE WOMEN: Usually by bronzing them. So whether you're 5'1" or 5'2", let me turn you into a statuesque beauty. Silver and gold plate also available. No credit cards.

DOUBLE YOUR PLEASURE: Siamese twins seek singular man who's not afraid of taking on life's challenges, or our mortgage payments. You cannot afford to pass up this incredible two-for-one offer. That's right. We're looking for just the right man to come between us. Romantic type preferred with no present attachments. Call and join us tonight. Actually, we're already joined, so just come over!

WILLING TO DATE BENEATH ME: Suicidal, despondent, psychotic, with M.B.A., currently living on ledge near top of the Chrysler Building, seeking like-minded distraught female, preferably blonde and beautiful, to share last fleeting moments of this unbearable life together. Don't be scared to plunge into a relationship! Tonight, from seventy-eight stories up, let's fall for each other. Smokers O.K. but no acrophobics.

WET AND WILD: My residence you've probably heard of, Marineland of the Pacific, but there's more to life than just a fancy address. I'm affectionate, warm-blooded, sensual, and can balance a ball on the end of my nose. Lately, all the males I've been meeting seem to belong to the same species, and I wind up getting in over my head. Write to me if you love art, appreciate seafood, and are a mammal. Children a possibility with advances in science. Waterproof photo a must! Scuba-diving equipment a big plus.

ANYONE WHO HAD A HEART: Would look at me, and know I need a transplant. Seeking a woman who can give me love, tenderness, and her heart forever. I'm sick of all these artificial relationships. I'm ready for the real thing. If you want our hearts to beat as one, don't wait another minute. Write c/o San Diego General Hospital. Hurry! I'll be heartsick if you don't!

PARANOID SCHIZOPHRENIC: I know I'm being persecuted by midgets in raincoats. And so do I. There are times when I can hear Volvo dealers mocking my porkpie hat. It makes me feel like doing nasty things. Me too. During the night, I can sense life insurance agents, disguised as Nazis, sneaking into my room just so they can soak my arch supports in sour cream. I hate that. Who can blame you? What I seek is an extrovert who loves to walk and—Wait, just you wait a minute. What I want is an introvert who loves to rent movies, cook—Never mind what he says! You have to be between 32 and 45 and also—Are you out of your mind!? Be 18–21 or be gone! You cradle robber! You necrophiliac! I hate you! Not as much as I hate you!! I could strangle you with my bare hands! They're my bare hands! No they're mine! Take this! Oh yeah! Take that! Take this! That! This!! That!! Arrrrgggghhh!!! By the way, nonsmoker preferred. I totally agree with you.

FED UP WITH BARS? So am I. What I'm looking for is a savvy, sophisticated female, 27–35, who can help spring me from this federal pen. A strong sense of humor and an interest in tennis or skiing are not as important to me as a knowledge of explosives and access to a helicopter. I'm fun-loving, tall and trim, currently serving twenty-five consecutive life sentences for robbery, murder, and attempted plagiarism of an Emily Brontë novel. Come any Tuesday between 1:00 and 2:00 P.M. But please don't wear plaid. It clashes with my stripes.

2B OR NOT 2B. THAT IS THE QUESTION: Because I can't remember what apartment I live in. Perhaps you can help me. My name is Al, uh no . . . it's uh Hal . . . Sal . . . Well anyway, I'm either 103 or 107 years old and I like younger women, 91–98, with good figures, good teeth, and good memories. If I sound like someone you know, please write and tell me who I am. Box number Q14 . . . uh, 8, no uh 39 . . . uh . . . What was I talking about?

AC/BC: Single, outgoing businessman, who looks considerably less than his 2,000 years, seeks stylish, stunning female, who appreciates the virtues of older men. Through the years, I've learned patience, understanding, and the meaning of commitment, from each one of my 257 wives. What I'm trying to say is that I've seen a lot. I was a witness to the fall of the Roman Empire, although, quite honestly, I would have much preferred to have arrived in the spring. All right. Now ask yourself this. Are you yearning for that special someone? Then write me soon. Because I know my love will last forever, even if you won't.

STRIKING BLUE-EYED MALE: Are you that special women to walk the picket lines with me? I am 70ish and have been striking the Birmingham Tool and Die company for the past 45 years, even though they went out of business in 1951. Enough of me. Who are you? That's simple. You have the hair of Marilyn Monroe, the eyes of Liz Taylor, and the body of George Meany. Just think, soon you can be in labor. Include photo and maybe some food stamps.

WHAT GOES UP: Impotent sales exec seeks woman for whom friendship is more important than sex. You are 16–106 years old, have never experienced an orgasm, and therefore won't miss them. Would like to hear from you, but don't have phone or mailing address. Contact me by skywriting. All responses kept confidential.

MATERIAL THINGS MEAN NOTHING TO ME: If they're worth less than $40,000. What I'm looking for is a man whose presence will always be welcome, providing it's gift-wrapped. Above all else, I believe that honesty is crucial to a relationship. It's true. I admit that I once turned down Aristotle Onassis's hand in marriage, but only after he didn't offer me the rest of his body. So come on. Let's unite our stocks and options and create a mutual bond. Please include photo, phone number, and credit rating. But don't bother writing if your bank account has less zeros than a Japanese fighter squadron!

HERPES FREE: That's right. There's no charge to you. I am a virile male who recently had a blood test and my doctor told me there's absolutely no doubt, I have blood. I can be dominant, submissive, or play the role of Ernest Borgnine, it's all up to you. Believe me, there's nothing, absolutely nothing that I wouldn't do to satisfy a woman, except give her pleasure. So don't let a condom come between us. More than anything else, I want to give everything I have to that special someone!

LET'S WOK AROUND THE CLOCK: Who are you? You are that mystical creature who works right across the street in that Szechuan laundry. I can see you right through my window because it's late afternoon, and the bus fumes have lifted. Oh, the aromas that waft up to my room every night! The tantalizing smell of sweet-and-sour shirts, starched shrimps and, my all-time favorite, stir-fried shorts. Dare I mention this? I even know your name. Ling Ring Ding. Yes, my dearest, I could tell immediately that you obviously have breeding. Thousands and thousands of roaches breeding in your kitchen right now, but I don't care. Because it's spring. Time to think of life, love, and my special place in the universe, which fortunately is rent-controlled. Yes, we can share it together and don't worry. By New York standards it's incredibly large. How large? Well, if it were five feet wider, it would be two-dimensional. But we can discuss all that later. Come, my little wonton. Come and cover my entire body in duck sauce. That's right. I want the whole neighborhood to hear me scream, "No MSG, oh God, please no more MSG!!!"

ADVANCED FOR MY AGE: I'm seven years old, currently in summer camp, but have been told I'm advanced for my age. Really I am. In fact, my mommy's even sewn a name tag into my diaphragm. O.K. I'd like to meet a professional, preferably a child psychologist, but absolutely no more than eight years of age. I'm bright, perky, petite, and weigh only fifty-three pounds, so I'm easy to take anywhere. Let's meet for a quiet, relaxed drink; however, I do have to be in bed by 8:00 P.M. No immature men. Please!

SOUTH AFRICAN FILM DIRECTOR: Forced to leave my native land because I wanted to shoot a documentary in black and white, but the government would only let me do it in white. I am looking for a woman to marry so that I can finally have love, happiness, and a green card. Please include recent photo, the best time to call, and proof of American citizenship.

COME CELEBRATE THE HIGH HOLY DAYS: And the low holy days. Manic-depressive rabbi seeks woman with Orthodox background in shock therapy. Friends describe me as the "Lennon" type or the "Lenin" type, who knows? Come, let's go and plant a tree in Israel, if we can find a shovel long enough. Let me tell you, bubby, I'm pretty sensitive, mostly because I got 50% off at my circumcision. All right, all right, listen. We'll relax, have a drink, maybe even smoke some matzoh together. Believe me, as it says in the Torah, we're all tourists in life till we reach our final destination. Oy, then try getting your luggage. So, if you have over five thousand years of Jewish blood running through your veins, tell me, don't you think it's time for a transfusion?

LET'S GET DIGITAL! Binary sexual seeks computer mate. You must have over 128K of memory and be available for random access. Looking for a relationship with maximum expandability. I'm IBM compatible and have been told by friends I've got a great pair of modems. Let's spend the night listening to the magical sounds of Brazilian logarithms. I dislike men who smoke, drink, or use cursor words. Let's exchange data. I can turn your software hard. This baby bytes! No men with terminal diseases, please!

MEN WHO HATE THEMSELVES: BY GIRLFRIEND'S BRA SIZE

38D	01%
48D	001%
58D	0001%
158D	*
36C	14%
34C	24%
32C	34%
22Q	**
34A	67%
28A	76%
1A	***
34B	50%

*Unfortunately, suffocated to death before he could answer.
**Unusual case: Seven breasts, twenty-six nipples, claims her name is Ann Dromeda.
***Boyfriend suffers from acute eyestrain.

CHAPTER 8

SAFE SEX IN THE EIGHTIES (OR HOW TO BE YOUR OWN BEST LOVER)—ADVICE FROM DR. BABY RUTH

"Some men want raw sex, others want it steamed."

So says Dr. Baby Ruth, a therapist who specializes in giving advice to immature men and women, i.e., members of the "Baby" boom generation. According to her, millions of men and women are turning off to sex altogether, especially when they're in the altogether. However, Dr. Baby Ruth suggests that even those who choose to remain celibate should take no chances and always wear a condom, even when masturbating.

The facts suggest that the choice to be alone comes to different people in different ways. Dr. Baby Ruth explains that she literally comes across hundreds of men who continue to be hung up because of a previous relationship. "Especially if the noose was strong," she adds.

From this, she goes on to talk about those men who take breakups very badly. Incapable of handling the pain, they frequently go out and get themselves thoroughly plastered, sometimes even painted or wallpapered. "Yes, you can die of a broken heart," Dr. Baby Ruth says. "But only if the aorta is involved."

THE CASE OF MILTON DRUBNER—VIETNAM VET

Now we hear from one of Dr. Baby Ruth's most famous cases, Milton Drubner, a Vietnam vet during the Nixon years, who gave shots to almost every poodle in Saigon.

"I've had a lot of problems with my sexual identity. I used to be a pederast, but since I went into therapy, I've been pedicured. Still, it's tough being a single guy. For a while I was going out with this lawyer, Sheila, but I never got a chance to sleep with her, even once, because she was always tied up in tubal litigation.

"After that fiasco, I got involved with this cocktail waitress, but she was so hyper that she did about 3500 sexual revolutions per minute. By this time, I was pretty down on the whole dating scene, but then I met this terrific Jewish girl, Melissa Schtupsky.

"I remember our first night together and the way Melissa screamed when we made love. 'Oy vay! Oy vay! Oy vay!—Not that vay!!' Since that night, we've spoken only on the phone, but for some reason she always puts me on hold to take obscene phone calls."

Although Milton has now completely withdrawn from sex, as well as a Comp Lit course he was taking in night school, he's redirected his energies toward more profitable avenues. Currently in the area of real estate, he's building a special group of oceanfront condos for intellectuals, now being offered to people with high I.Q.'s as "George Bernard Shores."

REALLY LOVED ONLY HIMSELF

Dr. Baby Ruth tells us of another one of her cases. A pathological narcissist named Ken who loved himself so much that he often sent himself flowers, candy, and once even an ankle-length pearl necklace. Now we hear his story through the words of his last girlfriend:

"Ken was so self-absorbed that, when you come to think of it, he was actually more of a Bounty towel than a man. It never failed. He loved to catch glimpses of himself in mirrors, store windows, hub caps, even those on moving cars. Also, sexually speaking, he was totally into himself, always forcing me to wear a special mask—one with *his* picture on it!

"Eventually, he decided that he didn't need a partner and chose instead to make love only to himself. It was pathetic. He would wake up in the morning and say, 'Was it good for *me* too?'

"I knew he was on the verge of a nervous breakdown the day he called and asked me if I knew a good lawyer, because he was thinking of slapping himself with a paternity suit."

Unfortunately, Ken was one of Dr. Baby Ruth's few failures. A conceited egotist to the very end, his last will emphatically stated that, for the edification of future generations, he wished to have his sex organs laminated and kept in a portfolio—a *very* large portfolio.

THE STRANGE CASE OF MICK VAH

Next we look into the unusual life of Mick Vah, a drifter who was not only one of Dr. Baby Ruth's former patients, but one of her ex-patients as well.

As it happened, his cousin Bernice decided to throw an Oscar party, and it was a wonderful success, despite the fact that only three guests showed up—Oscar de la Renta, Oscar Rubinstein, and seventy-eight-year-old Oscar Mayer, who walked in holding his wiener.

Yet this turn of events didn't discourage Mick from mingling with his cousin's guests, for he was really quite adept at breaking the ice. It was a social skill that would have been more than welcome had he not also been adept at breaking the rules of grammar, the furniture, as well as a few arms.

Well, this show of temper led him to be quickly ejected from the gathering and, in a moment, he found himself on the front lawn, unceremoniously sprawled at Lola's feet.

Luscious Lola Victrola.

Ask anyone who knew her and they would tell you that Lola simply radiated sex, especially after her illicit weekend at Three Mile Island. A scandalous affair, she had been caught redhanded by local church leaders as she attempted to help a muscular young priest celebrate critical mass.

But who could blame the poor devil? Lola's body exhibited so many dangerous curves that the state legislature, meeting in closed session, was forced to pass a special law requiring any man making love to her to wear a seat belt.

So, as Mick rose to his feet, it was this truly glorious feminine vision that filled his eyes. Feeling a rising hunger in his loins, he was instantly enthralled by the mesmerizing scent of Lola's exotic perfume, Eau de Hoboken.

Something in the Way She Smells

"Mmmm, the smell of her was soft and beguiling, a fragrance of orchids and lilacs, mysterious, yet not unlike a moonlit night in the midst of a Bombay landfill. What a delicious dish she was! I wanted her to be everything, my mistress, my seamstress, oh I didn't care, any kind of stress would do.

"Curse the cruel fates, curse them I say, for even as I poured out my feelings to her, she told me that her heart belonged to another—although, she added consolingly, there were still options available on her pancreas."

Predictably, Mick took her words as rejection and went on a three-day bender. However, it ultimately required six uniformed officers to get him to stop bending her. When Mick finally staggered into Dr. Baby's Ruth's office, all he had were the clothes on his back, a few crumbs of bread, and access to a fifty-million-dollar trust fund.

Why Dr. Baby Ruth Took the Case

Seeing the pitiful condition of the dilapidated young man made Dr. Baby Ruth realize that it would take years and years of therapy, meeting with him at least five times a week, before she could make a down payment on that mansion in Beverly Hills.

Indeed, this Mr. Mick Vah reminded her of another one of her famous cases: Ingrid, the Elephant Woman, who required three couches to lie down, but whose ability to pay $1200 an hour enabled Dr. Baby Ruth to purchase a Leer jet (a special low-flying plane that allows everyone on the ground to watch you making contemptuous faces at them).

Seeing how she could help this poor, tortured young man finally led Dr. Baby Ruth to accept Mick's case, but only on three conditions: that he promise to attend the sessions regularly, listen to her advice carefully, and pay cash in advance. They began to work together and immediately started making enormous strides. The following is . . .

An Excerpt from Dr. Baby Ruth's Notebook

"Today, Mick seemed unusually distraught. He confessed it had been a bad year. A year in which he had lost both his parents. But unfortunately, someone had found them. Why he hated them so was a mystery to me, because they were obviously supportive.

"Early on, they encouraged him in everything he wanted to do, particularly in his desire to throw himself in front of a bus. But, being dyslexic, he kept throwing himself in back of the bus, which left him even more of a failure in their eyes.

"A morose child, it took much probing to get him to speak about the time he purposely laid his whole body down in front of a speeding locomotive, only to wind up wrecking his Lionel trains. I don't believe I've ever seen a compulsive failure as neurotic as this one.

"Just before the end of our session, he described in great detail the horrible ordeal he went through when he tried to commit suicide by attempting to slash his wrists—with an electric razor.

"Every time I hear him speak, I realize there is so much more work to be done. Thank God. My apartment in Trump Towers definitely needs some renovations."

Miraculously, once Mick was able to break the barrier of talking about his parents, he made an unusually fast recovery, which occurred just a few days short of his twenty-sixth year in therapy. Even more amazing was that this psychological clean bill of health coincided, to the minute, with the exhaustion of his trust fund.

"The final breakthrough came when I got Mick to see that maybe, just maybe, his father had a right to complain that his work was always piling up on him," notes Dr. Baby Ruth. "After all, the man was a proctologist."

HOW TO GET YOUR OWN TV SHOW

At this point, Dr. Baby Ruth shares with us some of the unique insights she's offered through the years, especially to people who want to know how to get their own syndicated TV show.

"A Viennese accent doesn't hurt," she says candidly. "Believe me, I know. For I was born over sixty-five years ago in a seething ghetto just outside Raleigh, North Carolina, and I sounded even worse than Scarlett O'Hara. Let me tell you, it took years and years at the Sigmund Freud Speech Center before I was able to speak like a refugee."

MEN WHO HATE THEMSELVES: BY VISA CREDIT LIMIT	
5¢ or less	100%
67¢	99.9%
99¢	98.9%
$1.00	82.7%
$34.00	71.5%
$102.32	61.5%
$500.00	50.0%
$8401.99	42.8%
$75,000.00	20.0%
$75,001.00	14.9%
$5,361,948.17	08.7%
$49,006,299.99	03.4%
$868,943,736,400.75	01.2%
over $999,999,999,999,999,999.01	???*

*Michael Jackson refused to comment.

CHAPTER 9

DETERMINING A MAN'S H.Q. (HATE QUOTIENT)

NAME: ARNOLD HANS
AGE: 31
OCCUPATION: PROFESSIONAL LOOKALIKE FOR THE INVISIBLE MAN

Hates self because he never gets any recognition. Once passed a kidney stone, and it didn't even say hello.

NAME: CECIL MAHLER
AGE: 47
OCCUPATION: CERTIFIED PUBLIC ACCOUNTANT

Hates self because his wife Hattie, after twenty years of marriage, continually complains that he can only give her a "Boregasm."

NAME: MAURICE LONGO
AGE: 83
OCCUPATION: UNEMPLOYED DENTIST

Hates himself because, for the last fifty-seven years, he's been out of root canal work.

Boregasm

NAME: HARRY KRUTZ
AGE: 29
OCCUPATION: PURVEYOR OF ENVIRONMENTAL
         MERCHANDISE (UMBRELLA
         SALESMAN)

Hates self because his wife likes to sleep with a teddy and the bed gets really crowded—with him, her, and the senator from Massachusetts.

NAME: DOMINICK SHMUTZER
AGE: 67
OCCUPATION: JUNGIAN THERAPIST

Hates self because he's not as Jung as he used to be.

At first glance, all of these men apparently have confessed to hating themselves, but do they all mean the same thing? Unfortunately not. For most men have a habit of saying one thing when they mean another. Take for example Sherman Treblinka, of Omaha, who wrote us recently and complained, "I just can't stand myself anymore."

That was fine until, upon further examination, we found out that what he really needed was help getting up.

Naturally, our misunderstanding with Sherman caused us great concern, so we flew him in for an interview. It was amazing. All it took to gain this wonderful little man's confidence was love, patience, and some occasional glimpses at a cattle prod.

Sherman, while he was alive, helped us in learning much. For as precise as our interviewing process was, in a controlled environment devoid of minor distractions such as food and water, we learned that it was still possible to make errors. What was required was a precise and uniform way to determine—once and for all—how much a man really hates himself, especially in a bathing suit.

That's how H.Q. was born. It required extensive trial and error, and over fifteen minutes at a local McDonald's, but now here it is. An exam that a man can take in the privacy of his own home, even with friends, family, or his parole officer looking on.

Enough said. Are all you men out there ready to have a truly terrific time as you take a comprehensive in-depth look at every aspect of your life? Then you're taking the wrong test.

CAUTION: After taking this exam, some men might feel as though they're hopeless cases. Others won't be that optimistic.

O.K. Begin.

1. Which gives you the greatest sense of anxiety?
   a) Inflation
   b) Toxic waste
   c) Nuclear holocaust
   d) est graduates

2. When people first meet you, they treat you with:
   a) Respect
   b) Contempt
   c) Indifference
   d) Thorazine

3. Which is your favorite form of exercise?
   a) Pull-ups
   b) Chin-ups
   c) Sit-ups
   d) Throw-ups

4. At dinner, you sit:
   a) With your legs apart
   b) With your legs crossed
   c) With your eyes crossed
   d) Under the table

5. What's the last thing you've read?
   a) *War and Peace*
   b) *The Encyclopaedia Britannica*
   c) *Airport*
   d) The label on a bottle of sleeping pills

6. The kind of birth control you prefer is:
   a) The pill
   b) A diaphragm
   c) The rhythm method
   d) Not bathing

7. When you know you are right, do you:
   a) Strongly voice your opinion
   b) Logically assert the facts
   c) Gently try to persuade
   d) Apologize

8. You were brought up:
   a) In the city
   b) In a small town
   c) In the country
   d) In a petri dish

9. What is your major source of income?
   a) Stocks
   b) Real estate
   c) Nine-to-five job
   d) Check from Mother on your birthday

10. Your best friends would love to see you:
    a) A millionaire
    b) Happily married
    c) On *Lifestyles of the Rich and Famous*
    d) Dead

11. How do you react to unfair criticism?
    a) Ignore it
    b) Refute it
    c) Disprove it
    d) Agree with it

12. You get others to smile by:
    a) Doing impressions
    b) Telling jokes
    c) Clowning around
    d) Leaving

13. What you most would like to collect is:
    a) Famous paintings
    b) Abstract sculptures
    c) Rare stamps and coins
    d) Dust

14. Complete this famous song lyric:
    "Me am me and you are you and they are all _____"*
    a) In traction
    b) In trouble
    c) Indifferent
    d) In Cleveland

15. How many miles a day do you jog?
    a) 6,000
    b) 10
    c) Less than ¼ mile
    d) Take a taxi to the bathroom

16. What's your favorite kind of food?
    a) Mexican
    b) Chinese
    c) Lithuanian
    d) TV dinner sucked through a straw

17. The perfect environment for you would be:
    a) A Swiss chalet
    b) A French château
    c) An English manor
    d) A Turkish jail

18. Which is the closest to your astrological profile?
    a) Libra with Virgo rising
    b) Gemini with moon in Capricorn
    c) Pisces with a double Scorpio
    d) Pisces with a double Hernia

*O.K. O.K. But if we used the *real* lyric, we would have to pay *You Know Who* a lot of money.

19. If a TV series were based on your sex life, it would be:
 a) *The Six-Million-Dollar Man*
 b) *Have Gun, Will Travel*
 c) *Superman*
 d) *Emission Impossible*

20. The type of therapy that would most benefit you is:
 a) Group
 b) Primal
 c) Weekly analysis
 d) Euthanasia

ANSWERS: Questions 1–20 are all (surprise) "D." Now give yourself ten (5) points for each correct answer.

81–100

Congratulations! Unable to get a new lease on life, you settle for a sublet. In every way your loathing and contempt for yourself is completely justified. As a matter of fact, we've heard there's an excellent possibility that you will be asked to star in *The Geek Tycoon*. A film about a shipping magnate who gives up everything for the chicken he loves. All right. Let's face the facts the way they really are. You're a wretched, miserable, abject figure, but not a bad C.P.A.

61–80

Pretty good. Your feelings about your life tend to vacillate back and forth, alternating between complete shame and total guilt. But on the plus side, thanks to your family's wonderful genes, you'll never lose any of your hair, that is, the hair inside your nose. What's more, this score reveals that you hate yourself without any reservations, probably because a good hotel wouldn't give them to you anyway. But that's your trouble. You never plan ahead. The only thing you've got saved for a rainy day is $3.42, and a picture of Lorne Greene in a kimono. Don't worry. We won't ask you why.

41–60

Not bad. You take a pretty dim view of yourself, probably from not paying the electric bill. The only occupation you could possibly find is working as a small-time hood—over a Volkswagen engine. And as if all that wasn't bad enough, you have a tendency to grow petulant, which is often quite difficult, considering the soil and temperature. O.K. To sum it all up, in the Great Supermarket of Life, you're standing on the express checkout line.

21–40

Extremely poor. This score reveals that a lot of work needs to be done. Essentially you're an emotional kind of man, the type who likes opening himself up completely to women, though most would still prefer not seeing your internal organs. However, on a more upbeat note, you have been shown to have great distaste for yourself. So much so that, on one occasion, you went down the block and had your tongue Scotchgarded. Don't worry. There's still a lot of hope. Because when it comes to heredity you're right down there, at the shallow end of the gene pool!

0–20

You're a disgrace! No doubt your positive attitude comes from an overprotective family who, when you were growing up, kept you behind barbed wire. Oh why can't you be a real man who hates himself!? Someone who's not ashamed to stop, take a moment, and smell the mildew. But no, not for you. You're the type who takes all the vitamins and minerals your doctor recommends and then claims to be completely rejuvenated, even though you weren't Jewish to begin with. It's no use. The odds are completely against you. You'll never *ever* hate yourself. Pathetic!

MEN WHO HATE THEMSELVES:
BY COLLEGE MAJOR

Chemistry	42%
Botany	41.7%
Art History	99.4%
English/Comp Lit	99.9%
History	50.1%
Pre-law	17%
Pre-med	.003%
Psychology	100%
Journalism	101%
Business	.02.1%
Political Science	34.7%
Philosophy	200%

CHAPTER 10

LIVING, LOVING, AND LOATHING

Most men, according to our survey, said they would love to enter a matrimonial state, just not one with community property laws. However, when you question them more deeply, you find that almost all of them are cynical, disenchanted, and upset, not only with themselves, but with the latest episodes of *Miami Law*.

Of course, some men only begin to hate themselves after spending an entire weekend with a woman, or after spending an entire paycheck, whichever comes first. What we discovered through the course of our interviews was that many men found themselves invaded by a profound sense of sadness, a longing to return to a more innocent time, but generally no earlier than 3:00 P.M.

In another important area, there was almost universal accord, because most of the men we interviewed agreed that sex was turning out to be more trouble than it was worth, especially when it wound up costing more than a hundred dollars an hour, plus tip.

The bottom line is: What can these men do? Who can they turn to? In our next study, we'll find out.

EDGAR THE FLIRT DOES HIS WIFE DIRT

"Edgar loved to flirt at parties, except he wouldn't flirt with women, only inanimate objects. Often, he'd wink at centerpieces, amuse silverware, and once I even caught him in the cloakroom, fondling a tureen of soup.

"He would claim that his flirtations were innocent and harmless, but after I caught him in a Howard Johnson's under an assumed name, and in the arms of a chair, I knew I could never trust him again."

Edgar's wife finally divorced him, some years later, after she found him in a compromising position with a spittoon.

Caught red-handed—in the arms of a chair!

He begged her to forgive him but she would have none of it, preferring instead to spend the remaining years of her life holding hands with a clock.

This decision crushed Edward, and he wondered about his wife's rationality, since the clock was digital. But like a lot of men whose wives leave them, in order to cope with the pain and suffering of a failed relationship, Edgar decided to pull himself together and wash that woman right out of his toupee.

Yes, there are all sorts of people who are incompatible, and they always seem to find each other. In the next case study, we focus on a man who loved to immerse himself in relationships, unfortunately, he couldn't swim.

THAT AMANDA—HE JUST CAN'T STAND HER!

"When I look back, I don't ever remember Amanda being supportive, except once, before I tried out for the Martha Graham troupe, when she offered to help me into my leotard with a spatula.

"Her sarcasm was really annoying, and not only that, she was always reprimanding me. But when she ridiculed me for playing strip poker with my file cabinet, man, that was the straw that broke the camel's back and I really told her off.

"Well, you know what she did?

"She sidestepped the whole issue and simply said that I looked anemic. 'Oh yeah,' I retorted. 'It just so happens that my parents were born in this country!' I guess that showed her."

THE TWO MAJOR REASONS COUPLES DESPISE EACH OTHER

Sex and money are the two major reasons that couples grow to despise each other, followed closely by money and sex. In the following case study, a man and a woman grow increasingly critical of each other, their lives, and certain Swedish movies. Moreover, they find themselves subject to the criticism of their children, which is even made more tragic by the fact that they never had any. Hear it from the lips of Jerry's wife:

"Our sex life together was becoming pretty infrequent. In fact, toward the end, we only made love once every four years, and even that was just during presidential inaugurations.

"You know. It was only after we were divorced that I found out that Jerry was having lots of extramarital affairs, often throwing weddings and bar mitzvahs for people he didn't even know.

"Let me tell you, it was a nightmare living with him. Mostly because he was so cheap. Once he bought a new copier for the office, and you know what, it turned out to be a monk."

Was Premarital Sex the Hex?

The potential breakup of any relationship is always sad. However, when you examine all the issues, perhaps the ultimate cause of Marge and Jerry's problems was the fact that they both believed in premarital sex—only not with each other.

In the professional, workaday world, we found that many men and women just didn't have time to cultivate a relationship. And when they did, often the results were not up to expectations.

THE PHOTOGRAPHER WHO
EXPOSED HIMSELF

Take the case of Gregory. A top photographer, he experimented with a revolutionary new technique for five years, but was bitterly disappointed when critics suggested that he might achieve better results if he took the lens cap off the camera.

Undaunted, he went out and bought rolls and rolls of film and then proceeded to butter them, until a friend explained that the basic idea was to put the film inside his Nikon. It was a revelation.

For Gregory always knew that he would become a great and sought-after photographer because, and this was his good fortune, he had perfect WASP features, with large antennae coming right out of his forehead.

Since his work was primitive and incomprehensible, he was immediately hailed by SoHo's most prestigious gallery owners as a genius. At one of his gala photography openings, in which he featured film that had been exposed for more than forty-eight hours (to educational television), he met a woman who was to dominate his thoughts as no other.

A Lawyer Named Sue

"What an extraordinary woman she was! Over a period of just three months, she underwent fifty-seven miscarriages —luckily, they were only of justice.

"Sue, my little Sue, that woman knew exactly how to turn me on! I loved it when she slipped into her legal briefs and paraded in front of me, covering her breasts with flimsy subpoenas, while her voluptuous vulva was provocatively shrouded by show cause orders.

"Things were so good between us.

"She only objected if I couldn't sustain myself. There I was, all ready to court her, but then the unthinkable happened. She ran off with a well-hung jury. It was that day I decided to give up photography and concentrate on passing the bar.

"But I couldn't pass it, so instead I went in and got drunk."

The yearning and desire for a truly meaningful love involvement is the one thing that continues to bring men and women together, although some credit has to be given to those free passes for discos. But some people travel far and wide to find the right person for them, or the wrong person, if it's getting too late. Such a place is that romantic and legendary retreat that caters exclusively to those men and women who want only to become doctors.

IT HAPPENED AT CLUB PRE-MED

It was there that Paul and Diane met. He had been a "hip" journalist for *Rolling Stone,* but was summarily fired when it was discovered that he had almost no knowledge of knees, ankles, or thighbones. And Diane, she had gotten into medical school through the back door, since her father was the janitor.

On the very first night, they danced. Paul swept her up in his arms, and, just a little while later, they sneaked away to take a series of x-rays together. Soon they were exchanging specimens. It was magical.

"There we were, Paul and me, running free on a nude beach, our stethoscopes intertwined, oh, it was too divine! We had our own little oxygen tent on the beach and piña coladas were brought to us regularly by friendly native orderlies.

"But perhaps the most romantic night of all was our last on the island. There we were, under the moonlight, slowly

Club Pre-Med

gorging ourselves on bed-pan fried liver. Our I.V.s reflecting the emerald-green Caribbean sea. Oh yes, that man could do things with a tongue depressor that would make Masters and Johnson tingle!

"However, the prognosis for our relationship changed radically when we got back to the States. Because now, before we made love, he had me sitting in his waiting room. At first it wasn't so bad, the waits weren't more than five or ten minutes.

"But then I found myself waiting for over an hour and you know what, he was seeing other lovers before me, even though they didn't have an appointment.

"I was hurt. Humiliated even further by my health plan, which sent me a form letter stating that I couldn't use my relationship with him as part of the deductible. Finally, I begged him, I pleaded with him, 'How can I ever, ever cure myself of this love I feel for you?'

"He didn't say anything for a long moment, but instead just looked deeply into my eyes. Then he took my hand in his and asked, 'So, are you allergic to penicillin?' The cad!"

SHEILA, JEANNETTE, BEATRICE, AND MERV

Yes, living, loving, and loathing, it's been the way of relationships since the dawn of time. You meet someone, you fall in love, and you wind up hating them for the rest of your lives, or the rest of your afterlives, if you're Buddhist.

There's no escape. Sheila Ostrow, of Topeka, married a guy whose sense of humor was so dry that she had to buy a humidifier. Jeannette Monroe, a weaver of jackets for cocktail franks, wound up with a maniac who treated her like dirt, and who was eventually arrested when he tried to forcibly fertilize the furrows in her brow. The list goes on and on.

Beatrice Schnoozer, a distraught young lady, came to us in the middle of her honeymoon with tears in her eyes, reporting that her husband, Alfonso, had come to their wedding bed and had attempted to deflower her while wearing a mask of Merv Griffin.

"Oh why, oh why, is he trying to gross me out!" she sobbed. We had to shake our heads and confess that we didn't know. Maybe it was cheaper by the gross.

MEN WHO HATE THEMSELVES:
BY CITY

Chicago, Illinois	34%
Secaucus, New Jersey	97%
Little Falls, Arkansas	12%
Newark, New Jersey	97.1%
Hollywood, California	00.2%
Hackensack, New Jersey	98.5%
New Orleans, Louisiana	23%
Hoboken, New Jersey	99%
Fairbanks, Alaska	01%
Trenton, New Jersey	99.7%
New York, New York	50%
Paramus, New Jersey	99.8%
Louisville, Kentucky	39%
Millburn, New Jersey	99.9%
Dallas, Texas	02%
Paterson, New Jersey	0%*

*Yeah, this kinda mystified us, too.

CHAPTER 11

PASSIVITY TRAINING FOR MEN

Are you the kind of man to demand a raise or promotion and get it? Even after you've been fired? Do you return defective jock straps six years later and still get triple your money back? Are you frequently the cynosure of all eyes at cocktail parties because of your wit, charm, and your ability to do fifty push-ups with your tongue?

Small wonder you don't hate yourself, alleges WIMP (Women In Male Positions).

You're a powerful and assertive man who knows exactly how to get your own way. And you probably have other bad habits as well. According to WIMP, it's clear that what you require is a good, weak dose of Passivity Training. A program especially designed so that no matter what the situation, any man can act with all the eloquence and forceful persuasiveness of a professional serf.

This is important. Because WIMP believes that true equality of the sexes can only be achieved in a society where women are totally dominant. And while WIMP is relatively small at the moment (only 215,875,334 members, and that's in Iowa alone), their numbers are rapidly growing.

Yes, WIMP is an aggressive organization that professes men will not be able to achieve true hatred of themselves

until they're subjugated, dominated, and forced to type over
sixty words a minute. Recently, the group proposed legisla-
tion that would give the electric chair to any man who
refused to handle diapers, laundry, or All-Temperature Cheer.

In all fairness, however, there is a liberal wing of WIMP
that feels that capital punishment is too extreme a punishment for men in these situations and, instead, suggests
merely imposing the death penalty.

WIMP MAKES HEFTY DEMANDS!

Furthermore, demands WIMP, if a man didn't have a hot,
nourishing supper waiting for his wife when she returns
home from work, he would automatically be given twenty-
five years to life at hard labor—or until he finally gave birth.
In addition, it would be absolutely compulsory for every man
to wear curlers in public, particularly at shopping malls,

and no exception would be made for men who were bald, either.

Finally, WIMP insists that $600 billion be set aside for research to perfect a pill that would not only give men incredible grace, poise, and sensitivity, but stretch marks as well.

This year, WIMP has developed a specific training program for Men Who Want to Hate Themselves even more, but first this.

THE RIGHTS OF PASSIVITY

1. A man has the right to beg forgiveness for each and every aspect of his behavior, especially when no apology is asked for.
2. A man has the right to submit to the sexual demands made by anybody of the opposite sex at any K-Mart
3. A man has the right to be fired without appeal. If his employer cannot find a reason for his dismissal, he is obligated to supply her with one.
4. A man has the right to be sold anything by any woman at any time; if he suspects that he's not being overcharged, he has the right to demand why.
5. A man has the right, in a physical confrontation with a woman, to get beaten up.

THE SIX BASIC SKILLS OF PASSIVITY

1. FORGETTABLE ASSERTION
2. SELF-DEPRECATION
3. NEGATIVE ACQUIESCENCE
4. UNSOLICITED REVELATION
5. AUTO-INTIMIDATION
6. ABJECT EUPHORIA

O.K. Let's see some WIMPs teach men the lessons they deserve!

Situation #1: Phil walks into the showroom of a used car dealership at exactly 7:30 A.M. and immediately sits down on a stool in the corner. At 4:48 P.M., he approaches the saleswoman.

PHIL: Excuse me.

SALESWOMAN: Yeah . . .

PHIL: Do you, uh, remember me? (FORGETTABLE ASSERTION)

SALESWOMAN: No.

PHIL: Of course not. I wouldn't expect you to.

SALESWOMAN: Listen, I'm busy. What is it?

PHIL: Nothing. Oh nothing. Nothing really. (AUTO-INTIMIDATION)

SALESWOMAN: It must be something.

PHIL: Well, I wasn't going to even mention it, but about that car I bought here yesterday, it—

SALESWOMAN: Car? Car? What car?!

PHIL: The . . . uh . . . tan station wagon.

SALESWOMAN: With the purple racing stripes?

PHIL: That's the one. What happened—and believe me, I still have absolutely no idea of what I did wrong—is that the transmission fell out. (SELF-DEPRECATION)

SALESWOMAN: You boob!

PHIL: I know. I was a fool to drive it out of the showroom.

SALESWOMAN: Now hold on, buddy. You ain't here to claim a warrantee or nothing like that, are you?

PHIL: How could you say such a thing? (AUTO-INTIMIDATION)

SALESWOMAN: You sure?

PHIL: Positive. (NEGATIVE ACQUIESCENCE)

SALESWOMAN: Hmmmmm.

PHIL: Hmmmmm.

SALESWOMAN: Hmmmmm. So you need a new car?

PHIL: Boy oh boy! That's incredible! You hit the nail right on the head! (UNSOLICITED REVELATION)

SALESWOMAN: See that '51 De Soto over there?

PHIL: The one that's burnt out?

SALESWOMAN: Yeah. Ain't she a beaut!?

PHIL: She sure is. (NEGATIVE ACQUIESCENCE)

SALESWOMAN: Come over here. Look at this. No Michelin radials.

PHIL: Great.

SALESWOMAN: No AM/FM radio.

PHIL: Terrific!

SALESWOMAN: And with this base sticker price, you also don't get these options: a heater, motor, transmission—

PHIL: What about a sun roof?

SALESWOMAN: OK. We won't throw that in either.

PHIL: Don't say another word! It's a deal!! (ABJECT EU-PHORIA)

Situation #2: The boss lady gives Dave a call at home on Friday night at 11:59 P.M.

DAVE: Hello.

BOSS LADY: You've got to come in tomorrow.

DAVE: But I'm getting married tomorrow. (FORGETTABLE ASSERTION)

BOSS LADY: Is it an emergency?

DAVE: Well, no. (AUTO-INTIMIDATION)

BOSS LADY: That settles that. Who are you marrying?

DAVE: Mildred Slotnick.

BOSS LADY: That slut!

DAVE: The same one. (NEGATIVE ACQUIESCENCE)

BOSS LADY: That broad's a public health menace.

DAVE: My feelings exactly. (UNSOLICITED REVELATION)

BOSS LADY: I'll tell you one thing, if you marry that tramp, don't even consider coming in Sunday.

DAVE: You're the boss. (AUTO-INTIMIDATION)

BOSS LADY: So that's your attitude, is it? Well, just for that, you're fired. And to offset the losses you've cost me, I'm not paying you your last six months' wages! Now, what have you got to say to that!?

DAVE: Well . . .

BOSS LADY: Well!?

DAVE: Well, it should be eight months. (SELF-DEPRECATION)

BOSS LADY: You are *some* negotiator. I shouldn't allow myself to be manipulated like this but, O.K., make it eight months.

DAVE: What a gal! (ABJECT EUPHORIA)

Situation #3: Barry has a meeting with his next door neighbor Gladys over the backyard fence.

BARRY: Afternoon, Gladys.

GLADYS: Afternoon, uh, what's your name?

BARRY: Never mind. (AUTO-INTIMIDATION)

GLADYS: Summer'll be here soon.

BARRY: It sure will.

GLADYS: It's gonna get real hot. That's why I hired a contractor to build me a swimming pool right by the fence.

BARRY: Great idea!

GLADYS: There's only one problem.

BARRY: What's that?

GLADYS: Those weeping willows you got over there.

BARRY: The ones over six hundred years old? (UNSOLICITED REVELATION)

GLADYS: Them's the culprits. They interfere with the sunlight coming over my yard. I don't like to swim in the shade.

BARRY: Neither do I. (FORGETTABLE ASSERTION)

GLADYS: So, if it's O.K. by you, I'm just gonna grab my chain saw and take those suckers down.

BARRY: The sooner the better. (NEGATIVE ACQUIESCENCE)

GLADYS: And you'll pay for the carting away?

BARRY: No problem.

GLADYS: Just one more thing.

BARRY: My house? (UNSOLICITED REVELATION)

GLADYS: It's an affront to the neighborhood.

BARRY: You know, I was just telling my wife the same thing. (SELF-DEPRECATION)

GLADYS: So, as a public service, I called my sister's demolition company to level it.

BARRY: Wow! That's terrific!! (ABJECT EUPHORIA)

MEN WHO HATE THEMSELVES: BY FAVORITE PET

Dog	08%
Hippo	71%
Sheep	47%*
Toad	93%
Aardvark	50%
Cornish hen	51.5%
Christie Brinkley	00.0000000001%
Muskrat	68%
Amoeba	02%
Skunk	97.9%
Viper	98.9%
James Watt	99.9%
Mandrill	33.3%
Womandrill	33.3%
Bald eagle	17%
Curly eagle	17.1%
Eagle that uses Minoxydil	17.2%
Praying mantis	85%
Atheistic mantis	58%

*May hate selves, but they certainly love their sheep!

CHAPTER 12

MEN WHO ARE THEIR OWN WORST ENEMY (AND OTHERS LESS FORTUNATE)

In her book *The Female Noodnik*, Mildred Tata, a radical feminist, concludes that men also have legitimate grievances and should be afforded exactly the same rights as any other decorative object. However, despite her extreme rhetoric, Mildred writes with remarkable eloquence about her own parents, whom she compares, quite favorably, to Steve and Idi Amin.

"I didn't always used to hate guys," she confesses in an early chapter. "In fact, I used to like them quite a lot, until I discovered they were also men. That came as quite a shock!"

Indeed, it took years of therapy for Mildred to recover from this early traumatic experience, but on her sixty-seventh birthday, she decided to throw caution to the winds, and she accepted a date with a French race car driver. But much to her dismay, the evening was to end in bitter disappointment—after she discovered that he suffered from Prix-mature ejaculation.

Following that debacle, things looked pretty bleak for Mildred, so she came to where most people with bleak lives eventually come—New York City. Seeking cultural enlightenment, she was immediately drawn to the opening of a political drama entitled *All My Sonys*.

The story revolved around a greedy Japanese industrialist who is ultimately driven to hari-kari after being confronted with the fact that, during World War Two, he made defective Walkmans.

Yet the real drama that night wasn't taking place on stage.

Because it was there, during intermission, that Mildred Tata met Tony Aggiada, a New England mafioso, upon whose small and violent life she was to have a profound, if not minimal, effect.

238 POUNDS OF STEAMED MAINE MOBSTER

"Before I met Mildred, I was the best in the racket. I could knock over a bank in fifteen minutes, a trash can in ten.

"Nobody stood up to me.

"As a matter of fact, there was this one wiseguy who had gotten himself engaged and, on top of that, in trouble with the mob too. Well, I had no choice. I had to put out a pre-nuptial contract on him.

"Yeah, those were the days.

"But Mildred changed all that. She made me insecure. So insecure that my buddies started referring to me as a 'Lack of Confidence Man.'

"She, with her college degree, checking and rechecking the spelling of each little ransom note I sent. Forcing me to order cement shoes that met the current building codes.

"Yeah, according to her, I was an embarrassment to the human race, lazy, shiftless and cruel, although she once confessed that I made a passable Beef Stroganoff."

One day, after Tony started extorting money from Mildred's mother (allegedly to produce an autobiographical film called *20,000 Colleagues Under the Sea*), it dawned on her that he would just never change, so she packed her bags and left, moving in the next day with the noted producer of the hit TV series *Good Morning, Uganda*.

And poor Tony, without Mildred's benevolent guidance, he quickly ran afoul of the feds and was ironically shot down outside a local movie theater. No, the theater would never play his film.

What was showing was a movie starring Sonny Bono as a mad scientist who clones the woman he loves. Up on the marquee, the title of the film shown out brightly: *Cher and Cher Alike*. It was the last thing that Tony ever saw.

However, unlike Tony, some men who are their own worst enemies are seen by many on the outside as altruists. Like Wally Esperanto, an entrepreneur who invented a revolutionary new product for women called the I.O.U.D., which was essentially a birth control device bought on the installment plan.

A millionaire by the age of twenty-one, Wally met Molly, a professional pasteurizer of camel cheese, at a party given by a mutual friend, and a few weeks later they moved in together.

MOLLY REMEMBERS WALLY FONDLY

"Wally was a very concerned type of guy, you know, very charitable. When I first met him he was planning to throw a party for the homeless, although he later gave up on the idea when he realized how hard it would be to send them all invitations.

"He had incredible insights.

"When we first started dating, I had already been bulimic for a period of five years, yet somehow had managed to gain over three hundred pounds. It was Wally who taught me that you have to stick your fingers down your throat after you eat, not before.

"So you can see how gentle and sweet he was.

"Listen, I really don't understand what happened, but we kind of drifted apart. So much so that, toward the end, the only way we could communicate was with signal flags.

"Look, I bear the guy no animosity, just some papers from Marvin Mitchelson."

Even today, gentleman that he is, Wally only expresses the warmest recollectons of Molly. "She had a great sexual appetite," he says fondly. "And always insisted on keeping Raisinets, Oreos and Clark Bars within six inches of the bed. I miss her."

EVIDENCE PROVES NICE GUYS FINISH LAST

Studying the relationships of guys like Wally proved over and over again that nice guys finish last, especially in bed, where they usually finish several days after their partner leaves. In addition to this, further compounding the feelings of mistrust between the sexes, there were several instances we uncovered of women trying to take advantage of men who were extremely impressionable.

Thelma Dove, one night at a singles' party, encountered a young artist so impressionable that she immediately noticed there were literally thousands of people's fingerprints all over his body. Yet for Selma, it was like a dream come true. But allow her to describe the experience in her own words, or if not in her own words, then in someone else's.

A Psycho-Ceramic Relationship

"Edgar was perfect for me, I can't deny it, because I had been seeking a man for a long time that I could mold. So first I molded him into a flower vase, then into some pottery, and finally into a statue of Zeus.

"Well, our relationship was going along just great until that fateful day last October when he fell off the shelf. Hey—what can I say—it was a shattering experience.

"Ever since that moment, my life has completely revolved around Edgar's well-being. I've done everything in my power to pick up the pieces but, well, you know, it's tough living with a broken man."

Men who are their own worst enemy seem to come in all shapes and sizes, although many places seem to be temporarily out of size 9. They can be the boy next door, and sometimes even the girl next door, after a few discreet operations. Still others can possess phenomenal amounts of wealth.

A powerful international industrialist, who freely confessed being his own worst enemy, recently said to us, "Listen folks, I have all the money I could ever need. As a matter of fact I could retire tomorrow, if I moved to Sri Lanka."

As you can see, it's extremely hard to stereotype this particular category of man, although, oddly enough, it's not that difficult to monotype him.

Time after time, because of their insecurities, neuroses, and anxieties, the relationships these men have with their women wind up being torn asunder, or should it occur during the evening, they wind up being torn amoonder.

The point is, and this is a difficult issue to confront, that millions of women from every part of the land are finally deciding that their love objects are just not worth it, particularly if they use more than two batteries.

As Sally Mineola, a longtime resident of Dallas, phrased it so eloquently last week on the *Phil Donahue Show,* "I spent my entire life refining him, and now all I have left is a quart of motor oil."

Given all these adverse circumstances, it's amazing that any relationship can get off the ground at all. Yet here and there, we continue to hear of some rather naive men who actually believe they can make a relationship work. Al Bania is one of these.

ESMERELDA GOES AFTER HIS PITCH

"I recall when I first met Esmerlda at the Baseball Hall of Fame. She was witty, vivacious, intelligent, creative and charismatic. What can I say, I guess opposites attract.

"She batted her eyes at me and soon after that, she was batting clean-up for the Yankees. What a throwing arm she had! She was Mickey Mantle, Willy Mays, and Reggie Jackson all rolled into one, weighing in at about 945 pounds.

"Oh what curves she had! What screwballs! And what a sinker!

"I remember what used to get her really excited was the prospect of making love in an open field, but only if the Dodgers were playing on it at the time.

"Looking back, I guess I'll never totally understand why I struck out with her. Maybe I should have used more resin."

MEN WHO BLAME THEMSELVES

It's amazing. Some men will always blame themselves when things go wrong. A teller in Idaho blamed himself for the failure of his last seven marriages, the failure of his bank, as well as the failure of the latest Middle East peace initiatives.

This very same man, for some obscure reason, blamed himself for the wholesale slaughter of the Cherokee Indians and felt, had he only been there to intervene, that the whole thing could've been done retail.

Now, before we conclude, let's see if we can identify some other common characteristics of Men Who Are Their Own Worst Enemy. Here are some initial observations we've made, primarily because these guys wouldn't give us the other letters of their names.

MEN WHO ARE THEIR OWN WORST ENEMIES ARE:

1. **True Humanitarians.** Again and again, you will observe that their hearts go out to the world, although they never seem to use enough postage.

2. **Formidable Gourmets.** Quite often of the first order (or the second order if the restaurant is out of what they want). Point of interest: They are known to favor rack of Spam.

3. **Somewhat Ambivalent.** There is no doubt that they enjoy beating around the bush, a tendency the President's aides are trying more and more to discourage.

4. **Musically Inclined.** When surveyed, their favorite performer, without a doubt, is Felonious Monk (a rogue accordion player currently serving twenty-five years to life in Sing Song for murdering an innocent Melody).

5. **Mathematically Gifted.** Keen on figures, particularly women's, they like to come full circle, multiplying the radius by pi to figure out their sperm count.

6. **Literally Hermaphrodites.** In fact, many claim they get periods once a month—often into sentences which already contain a question mark or exclamation point.

7. **Immensely Egotistical.** According to recent studies, they have been known to announce over 327 times a day, "I couldn't have done it without me."

8. **Yet Strangely Modest.** They truly don't believe there's anything wrong with self-deprecation, as long as they don't insult anybody important.

9. **Culturally Eclectic.** Remarkably informed, they will go out of their way to see a rare film, though once in a while they might be persuaded to see one that's well-done.

10. **Spiritually Attuned.** Not surprisingly, many have attended seminary schools where they were required to take sacred oaths of poverty and chastity (declarations very similar to the ones taken by writers of humor books).

11. **Extremely Sensitive.** On a Sunday afternoon, they can be seen strolling in the park where suddenly they'll spot a sparrow with a broken wing. Yet you can be assured, with almost no hesitation whatsoever, they'll reach down and break the other wing.

12. **Born Crusaders.** Frequently against cults, there are reports of those who have spent years of their lives attempting to deprogram victims of the Moonies, Krishnas, and NBC.

13. **Controversial Speakers.** North to south, east to west, they tend to stir passions wherever they go by virtue of their extremely libertine attitudes, especially toward parking tickets.

14. **Tragic Figures.** All but unknown to the general populace, there is a shockingly high mortality rate among those men accidentally strangled by barbells (a controversial topic soon to be the theme of a major motion picture entitled *Pumping Irony*).

15. **Middle Aged.** Through our research, we discovered that most of them belonged to an exclusive organization called "So Happy I Turned 40!" or, as it's more commonly known, "SHIT-40!"

MEN WHO HATE THEMSELVES: BY FAVORITE MOVIE

Patton	01%
High Noon	01%
True Grit	01%
An Unmarried Woman	99.888%
Deep Throat	25%*
Midnight Cowboy	50%
The Graduate	50%
Little Big Man	50%
Casablanca	00.0000031%
Gidget Goes Hawaiian	107.45%
Little Caesar	.001%
Little Women	100%
North by Northwest	11%
South by Southwest	11%
East by Eastwest	110%
Friday the 13th	45%
Friday the 13th Part II	46%
Friday the 13th Part III	47%
Thursday the 28th	98.0003%

*Mostly they hated themselves because they weren't in it.

CHAPTER 13

A DAY IN THE LIFE OF A MAN WHO HATES HIMSELF

AM

8:00   Agnes drops by to talk about their relationship.
8:05   Only five minutes go by and already she's boring him.
8:06   With a drill.
8:07   Agnes leaves.
8:10   Goes to mirror. Stands in front and ridicules himself.
8:11   Now his body is rid of cules.
8:12   Just what are cules anyway?
8:17   A brilliant idea. Yes.
8:20   He'll mail himself bomb threats.
8:21   Forgets his address.
8:22   Day not starting out well.
8:30   Will nothing go right?
8:31   Or left?
8:32   Not if he doesn't get his wheels realigned.
8:45   Decides he wants a relationship with no strings attached.
8:48   Symbolically burns Agnes's Tampax.

9:00   Heartache. Realizes that he has no friends.

10:00   No family.

10:01   No clean shirts for tomorrow.

10:15   But manages to keep his appointment with the periodontist.

10:17   They engage in heavy bondage.

10:43   Comes home. Tongue-tied.

10:45   Looks at his hairline in the mirror.

10:46   No wonder his reputation has always *receded* him.

11:01   Thoughts of Agnes again.

11:02   The time she deflated his football.

11:03   Burnt his baseball.

11:04   Crushed his Ping-Pong ball.

11:05   Gee, what a ball-buster.

11:14   All right. Time to go out and buy the paper.

11:19   Accosted by panhandlers on the street.

11:21   He finally gives in.

11:22   And buys a few pans.

11:30   Back home again. What a life.

11:31   You're alone when you're born.

11:45   Alone when you die.

11:58   And alone when you live in a studio apartment.

11:59   O.K. Time for lunch.

PM

12:00   Maalox on a toasted bagel.

12:01   Nausea.

12:02   Vomiting.

12:03   Throwing up.

12:05   Yes, he definitely makes it better than his mother used to.

12:45   Keeps therapist appointment.

12:50   Talks about his father.

12:51   Who got 3–5 at Leavenworh.

12:52   And then 5–10 at Woolworth.

12:55   High school. Good memories.

12:56   Where he excelled at the sixty-yard dash.

12:57   The eighty-yard question mark.

12:58   Plus he could also draw an exclamation point over three stories tall.

12:59   But no one cared.

 1:00   Breaks down and starts to cry.

 1:01   Confesses that whiskey is ruining his life.

 1:02   Therapist suggests scotch instead.

 1:03   Session over.

 1:04   Suddenly feels guilty about his sister. A former professor.

 1:18   Visits her at mental institution.

 1:19   They stroll along a psychopath.

 1:25   She screams, "Eureka!"

 1:26   Probably because he forgot to shower.

 1:27   Is he being too sensitive?

 1:28   Closes his eyes.

 1:30   Remembers being dumped by Agnes.

 1:31   In a Hefty bag.

 1:32   The feelings of humiliation come back.

 1:33   So do all his résumés.

 1:34   Funny, he never sent any out.

 1:35   Kisses sister good-bye.

 1:36   Now wait a minute.

 1:37   Wasn't he an only child?

 1:38   No time to think about that now.

 1:53   Grabs a snack at the local diner. Relaxes.

 1:54   And dreams of the perfect date.

 1:55   The perfect fig.

 1:56   The perfect avocado.

 1:57   Becomes emotionally involved with a Greek salad.

 1:59   Check comes. Salad is gone forever.

 2:03   He'll never see his olive again. Oh well.

 2:10   Back to apartment.

2:11	Decides to relieve tension by masturbating.
2:12	Arms too short.
2:13	More frustration.
2:14	Goes to bathroom and glances in mirror.
2:15	Squeezes blackhead.
2:16	Stevie Wonder screams.
2:17	Whoops, wrong bathroom.
2:20	What a day, what a day.
2:23	Time to weigh his options.
2:24	They come out to slightly less than a pound.
2:29	Insight. Realizes that he's carrying a lot of emotional baggage.
2:30	The kind not even Eastern will check.
2:45	Desperation. Experiments with a mood-altering drug.
2:56	Enters another reality.
3:00	Not unlike Buffalo.
3:12	All right. All right. Maybe he's not living up to his full potential.
3:19	Further misgivings about his Agnes.
3:20	She's really driving him crazy.
3:21	And it's such a short drive.
3:22	He could probably walk it.
3:24	Must distract his thoughts.
3:26	Picks up book. Sits down and reads about the Vikings.
3:30	Seems that they traveled in vessels with high sterns.
3:31	Usually Dr. and Mrs. Stern, from Chicago.
3:32	Who also provided the Smorgasbord.
3:33	Fed up with history.
3:37	A thought crosses his mind.
3:38	But the light is red.
3:39	It gets killed.
3:42	Why is life so unjust?
3:43	We live.
3:44	We die.
3:45	We miss half-price sales.
3:46	Luckily, there's always TV.

3:47	Goes over. Switches on the educational channel.
3:48	Seems to be an opera about some auto transmission guys.
3:49	*Carmen.*
3:50	Switches off the educational channel.
3:51	Decides to watch film instead.
3:52	A cross between *Wheel of Fortune* and a Woody Allen movie.
3:54	*Vanna and Her Sisters.*
3:55	Definitely time to sell TV.
3:57	Agnes calls. This time to really tell him the score.
3:58	Lakers 68, Knicks 74.
4:00	Oh no! Old emotions come back.
4:02	Must bottle up emotions.
4:03	Bottle breaks.
4:04	Loses deposit on bottle.
4:05	Is there no hope?
4:06	Or chance of salvation?
4:07	Or towels in the bathroom?
4:15	Notices he looks a little pale.
4:20	Off to the tanning center.
4:27	Arrives.
4:29	Almost turned into pair of leather pumps.
4:30	Should've looked at Yellow Pages ad more closely.
4:40	Walks back home.
4:44	Surprise visit from old girlfriend.
4:45	So, after all these years, she still carries a torch for him.
4:46	A blowtorch.
4:48	Why are relationships always so complicated?
4:49	Not to mention the phone bill.
5:00	Distraught. Tries to blow brains out.
5:01	With a bellows.
5:30	Arms get tired. Really should do more push-ups.
5:31	Still determined. Opens medicine chest.
5:32	And swallows a bottle of sleeping pills.

Twenty years, and she still carried a torch for him.

5:33 Just the bottle, not the pills.

5:34 Can't seem to do anything right. Lies down.

5:35 A reflective moment.

5:37 True, death may be inevitable.

5:38 But it's certainly preferable to a weekend in New Jersey.

5:42 Is there no relief?

5:43 Certainly not in this year's Yankee bullpen.

93:78 Clock must be wrong.

5:53 Snack time.

5:54 Mmmm.

5:55 Mule livers.

5:57 Starts to put socks in alphabetical order.

5:59 What's this?

6:00 Discovers invitation to cocktail party.

6:01 Rush rush rush!

6:02 Arrives at cocktail party.

6:03   Spots a woman named Didi Vozzeli.

6:05   Says to her, "Funny, you don't strike me as Italian."

6:06   She hits him.

6:07   Leaves party.

6:11   Meets a gal at the bus stop who instantly lifts his spirits.

6:12   And his wallet.

6:13   Maybe he shouldn't have worn the Naugahyde leisure suit.

6:25   Home again. Sulks around the apartment.

6:30   Then the apartment sulks around him.

6:33   Life sulks.

6:47   Now he's desperate. Really desperate.

6:48   Calls suicide hot line.

6:50   Gets put on hold.

7:50   On hold.

8:50   On hold.

9:50   On hold.

10:50   Tells them that he's going to slit his wrists.

10:52   They tell him that's a foolish waste of time.

10:53   He should hang himself instead.

10:54   Time marches on.

10:57   And so does *Newsweek*.

10:58   The end is in sight.

10:59   Of course. Because he's sitting on a mirror.

11:00   Dwells on the prospect that he's doomed for eternity.

11:01   Unless he gets out of advertising.

11:11   Opens window and yodels, "Bess, You Is My Woman Now."

11:12   "You can have her," Mayor Koch yodels back.

11:15   Yes, he almost forgot.

11:27   Remembers to circulate petition amongst his neighbors to have himself evicted.

11:30   Suddenly roof collapses.

11:31   Of mouth.

11:32   Well, at least today wasn't as bad as yesterday.

11:39   Agnes calls.
11:42   She's eloped with a professional soothsayer.
11:43   A man whom she loves because he can only say, "Sooth."
11:48   Oh the despair!
11:50   What can he do?
11:53   He's repugnant. Vile and reprehensible.
11:56   That's right. He has no business living among decent folk.
11:59   Moves to Venice Beach, California.

MEN WHO HATE THEMSELVES: BY FAVORITE AUTHOR

Shere Hite	100+%
Gloria Steinem	100%
Betty Friedan	99.9%
Norman Mailer	.01%
Ernest Hemingway	.001%
James Joyce	65.2%
Gore Vidal	62.1%
Truman Capote	62.1%
Tom Wolfe	32.7%
William Shakespeare	51.9%
Edgar Rice Burroughs	02.0%
Jackie Collins	72.3%
John Clancy	21.6%
Erica Jong	84.4%
Woody Allen	*

*Statistically insignificant—only hates himself.

CHAPTER 14

THE HATE REPORT (PLUS CHERI HATE'S HATE MALE)

Has success spoiled Cheri Hate? We tried to ask her, but this was the message we got on her answering machine: "Hello. This is Cheri. If you were really a close friend of mine, you'd have my private number. Good-bye!"

But where does all this arrogance come from?

As you no doubt know, *The Hate Report* is one of the most profound and controversial books to have come out in the past quarter-century, for it has already incited women from around the country to march and demonstrate for immediate change, the most radical of which is changing the word "menopause" (clearly a sexist term) to the more socially correct "womenopause."

Naturally, we have to put Cheri's life in the proper perspective.

Throughout her childhood in New York, she was traumatized by an older brother who was a real lunatic. One day, just before he was going to be locked up in an insane asylum, he escaped and a few minutes later raped a terrified woman.

Cheri only found out about the incident after taunting classmates showed her the *New York Post* headline: "NUT

BOLTS, AND SCREWS!" It was a mortifying experience, and for years afterward Cheri regrettably found, try as she might, that she could only reach orgasm with hardware salesmen.

Once we understand this, it's easy to understand how her other attitudes toward sex evolved.

THE RIGHT TO FREEDOM OF ORGASM

"I feel I have a right to an orgasm, and it's a very political question for me. That's why, when I engage in sexual congress, it's always by two-thirds majority, with the full senate looking on."

Additionally, since Cheri is opposed to all forms of male immorality, particularly those practiced by men at the highest levels of government, she's now petitioning to immediately have the "Vice" taken out of Vice-President.

CONFRONTING THE ISSUES

All things considered, there's little doubt that Cheri is the kind of woman who makes it a big point to confront all the issues. Recently, during a visit to her local newsstand, she went directly over to the magazine rack and confronted an issue of *Life,* berated an issue of *Newsweek,* and then told the October issue of *Reader's Digest* exactly what she thought of it.

The encounter quickly became extremely volatile and police were promptly called to the scene when she stopped confronting—and started clawing—the swimsuit edition of *Sports Illustrated.*

After this incident, Cheri found that her notoriety had grown to such a point that she was being followed around everywhere by paparazzi, and in some cases, mamarazzi. Not having any privacy was taking its toll and she was fast becoming a recluse, although there were those less generous in the press who characterized her condition as being a loose wreck.

So Cheri moved to a high-security luxury building on New York's fashionable East Side. And that's where she met Carl.

CARL HEARD CHERI WAS A FABULOUS LOVER

Carl, her next-door neighbor, heard that Cheri was a fabulous lover, mostly because the walls were so thin. They saw each other for the first time on a beautiful spring day in late December. Both of them, feeling a little lazy that morning, were trying to flag down a limo to the laundry room.

However, limos being a little hard to find indoors, they both decided to throw caution to the winds and share a seat on the bus. Soon, it wasn't long before they were sharing everything, weekends in the country, candlelight dinners, cold sores. Wherever you went, they were the talk of the town.

And why not? Carl, who had been single his whole life, even when he was married, was absolutely infatuated with Cheri. He fixed her lamp, her couch, even her cat, and all with one pair of pliers. Yet there was serious trouble brewing in paradise.

Disturbing rumors began to circulate in the local newspapers that Carl had CIA and KGB ties. Now, that didn't bother Cheri at all, but those ties from Macy's, those were a disgrace.

And while Carl was obviously a man of extraordinary gifts, Cheri soon discovered that he had stolen most of them from orphans. So it soon became quite apparent, as her infatuation diminished, that she was willing to tolerate less and less.

CHERI BEGINS TO QUESTION CARL'S TASTE

Now, while she wasn't quite ready to say that Carl had no taste, various friends did begin to point out the fact that there was something a little bit curious about a man who loved to check in to hospitals, just for the food.

In addition to this, at various times, Carl was alternately convinced that he was Solomon, Moses, Einstein, Mel Brooks and sometimes all four. Various therapists had dismissed the symptoms as merely being a psycho-Semitic illness, but Cheri wasn't so sure.

Still, she tried everything to please him. On a Friday afternoon she went out and bought a new kind of diaphragm cream, one with only half the calories, but Carl didn't seem to notice. For he was the kind of man who made a distinct point to repress all his emotions, yet curiously never his pants.

Every day it seemed as if his psychological condition got worse.

Out of nowhere, he developed chronic insomnia. So he purchased a "White Noise" machine that was capable of drowning out the relentless traffic of the city with the sweet lullaby of waves, waterfalls, or the gentle sounds of Bill Buckley, purring.

Obviously the man was cracking up. Most of the time tension constricted his throat so badly that he could swallow no more than one strand of spaghetti at a time. Clearly, the handwriting was on the wall.

Cheri knew that, in order to preserve her sanity, she would have to leave him as soon as possible and yet, to her ultimate credit, she rejected him in truly poetic fashion— using iambic pentameter.

CHERI SWEARS AN OATH

That night she burned everything, pictures, mementos, presents, and—having put that dismal, failed relationship behind her—swore a solemn, sacred oath to herself. Never, never, would she ever give herself to another man.

Lend herself, perhaps.

So, fueled by the frustration of this experience, and also by several hundred Sara Lee pies, Cheri set out with a new spirit of purpose and determination to make her name even bigger than before, which she did quite rapidly, by having it injected with silicone. That's why today, in major newspapers and magazines across Nicaragua, you can see the results of these efforts in her syndicated column.

CHERI HATE'S "HATE MALE"

Dear Ms. Hate:
Annette, that's the girl I date, and me, that's the person Annette dates, were having a nice, low-key dinner at a place in our neighborhood that specializes in designer fish, Gucci Sushi. Anyway, completely out of nowhere, she starts screaming and yelling that I'm a misogynist. Well, I just couldn't believe my ears. Everybody knows how much I love miso soup. Who's crazy? She or I?
Confused

Dear Confused:
  You.

                                                        C. Hate

Dear Ms. Hate:
  I'm a writer myself. Recently, a friend of mine, who's a lifeguard at a secretarial pool, introduced me to Kathy. She's a terrific gal who can take over 160 words a minute —with her toes. I believe, after many years, I've finally found someone who can not only love, cherish and nurture me, but also take dictation as well. Does it sound like I'm her "type" writer?

                                                        Sincerely,
                                                        Norman M.

Dear Norman:
  The only type writer you are is an IBM (Ignorant, Boring Male). Listen pal, don't you remember we went out!? Don't you think I remember that you had a severe vowel disorder which manifested itself as a spastic semi-colon.
  Boy, what a physical mess you were, with your agonizing muscle spasms—which were followed by your oyster spasms and once even a clam spasm when we visited your parents in Coney Island. I can't believe that I stayed with you for so long. Even now, I still have the punctuation marks you left all over my body!

                                                        Cheri H.

Dear Ms. Hate:
  I'm a bum. A filthy, no-good, rotten bum. But that's not my problem. My problem is that I can only achieve erection in the back of freight cars. Is there something wrong with me?

                                                        Fondly,
                                                        Johnny Trash

Hobosexual encounter

Dear Mr. Trash:
    There's nothing wrong with you that's not wrong with every other guy I've ever met. You're a hobosexual—do you hear me!—a hobosexual! A man who can only get excited by women who are real tramps!!
                                                        Cheri

Dear Ms. Hate:
    Wait till you hear this. I found out that my husband Bud has been having an affair for the past sixteen years with three different women. Their names are—get this— Rose, Lily, and Daisy. What does this sound like to you?
                                                All My Best,
                                                Nadine

Dear Nadine:
    Sounds like Floral Sex. Boy, did you marry a lulu. I wouldn't be surprised if the next gal you caught him with was named Susan, but she'd have to be black-eyed. What is it with this Bud, anyway? I'll bet'ya he's a product of the sixties. A real flower child.

Not to bruise your feelings, or anything like that, but my guess is that as you're reading this letter he's probably pollinating some woman named Blossom right now, in your front yard, on top of a flower bed. Look at the bright side, honey. The guy's no shrinking violet. Maybe you can compromise. Work out a floral arrangement, or something.

Ms. Hate

Dear Ms. Hate:
   How can I tell if my girlfriend is frigid?

Embarrassed

Dear Embarrassed:
   See, after making love, if your sperm is frozen.

C.H.

Dear Ms. Hate:
   I'm Vice-President of the United States and I think I detect some hostility on the part of my wife. Last night, after making love, she turned to me and said, "Bentsen was right. You're no Jack Kennedy." What do you think she meant by that?

Sincerely,
Dan Q.

Dear Mr. Q:
   That you're no Jack Kennedy.

Cheri Hate

Dear Ms. Hate:
   My boyfriend Cliff is really into rock music, but I mean real rock music, the kind you make with rocks. Yeah, we went down to this rock festival and we heard vol-

canic rock, sedimentary rock, plus a rock opera by the Rolling Stones. It was totally outrageous.

Cliff bought me a lemon-and-limestone soda and then we really pigged out on marble cake. There's only one small problem. He really enjoys getting stoned a lot—only it's usually by angry mobs. To tell you the truth, I'm starting to feel a little petrified of him. You think there's any future for us?

Very Truly Yours,
Rock Bottom

Dear Miss Bottom:

No. When I was your age, I also went out with a disturbed rock musician who would sing to me, "Granite and Day, You Are The One." First he wanted me to move with him out to Boulder, next he wanted me to come to Pebble Beach, and finally, are you ready for this, he told me he was doing a book on the history of music, called Rock Formations, which he planned to write with a chisel. Well, to make a long story short, just like your boyfriend Cliff, this guy was full of schist.

C.H.

Dear Ms. Hate:

Sometimes I don't know about Bob. We'll be quietly walking down the street when, all of a sudden, he'll scream at the top of his lungs "On guard!" and start chasing some poor guy down the block with a sword. What kind of psychological problem do you suppose he has?

Concerned

Dear Concerned:

It's obvious. A duel personality.

Ms. C.H.

Dear Ms. Hate:
  You've got to help me! I've almost given up all hope. Over the last thirty years, I've been in England, France, Ecuador, Thailand, Brazil, you name it, even New Guinea. I've traveled the Torrid Zones, the Tropic of Cancer, all the while circling the equator and exploring every province and precinct on the face of the earth.
  That's right, in kingdoms, commonwealths, motherlands, and fatherlands, I've been looking for love. But the search has proven absolutely futile and now I'm at the end of my rope. You've got to give me the answer. I have to know right now. Tell me, oh God, please tell me! Where can I find the true meaning of love!?

Al

Dear Al:
  In the dictionary.

Cheri

MEN WHO HATE THEMSELVES:
BY FIRST NAME

Zeke	67%
Lefty	22%
Angelo	02%
Steve	34%
Tom	50%
Dick	51%
Harry	50%
Adolph	91%
Barry	87%
David	00%*
Elvis	17%
Nikita	43%
Oscar	99%
Herman	99.3%
Schlomo	99.9%

*Strange, isn't it?

MEN WHO HATE THEMSELVES:
BY WIFE'S FIRST NAME

Doris	46%
Karen	53%
Sheila	48%
Sharon	51%
Murray	1627%

CHAPTER 15

JANE FONDUE'S "AERO-PHOBICS FOR MEN"

Clark Barr, a resident of the Windy City, is so obese that when he wades into Lake Michigan for a dip, he winds up flooding Chicago. Donald Rump, a southern belle ringer, has accumulated so much extra poundage on his rear end that it requires a division of WACs just to spank him.

And Fatso Leibowitz, the man who invented the Full Metal Sports Jacket, holds the dubious honor of being so pathologically chubby that, the moment he starts to bossa nova, it registers 9.8 on the Richter scale.

Make no mistake about it. The wives of these men are plainly disillusioned with them and find it just a little bit stressful, to have their husbands while making love, raised and lowered over the bed with a forklift.

To answer the plight of these women, and of others who may be concerned their men are not quite in the shape they want, Jane Fondue has put together an excellent program. Specially designed to help gradually increase your man's heart rate—through anxiety attacks—to the point where it stops beating altogether.

HOW THE PROGRAM WORKS

It's simple. To start, men are required to report to exercise classes in which thirty women scream at them all at once, "I want a commitment!" You can believe us. It works wonders.

After that, a beautiful instructor with the face of Ingrid Bergman, the hair of Marilyn Monroe, and the figure of Raymond Burr leads things off with a series of warm-up exercises, and men are wholeheartedly encouraged to stretch their arms and legs, in addition to their credit limits.

Jane's instructors are all quite well trained and compassionate. They realize that Men Who Hate Themselves have traditionally shunned exercises that condition the heart, mostly because these guys probably didn't have a heart to begin with.

Nevertheless, just to be on the safe side, these same instructors are required during class to have each man check his pulse every five minutes—in the unlikely event he still has one.

ADVANTAGES OF AERO-PHOBICS

1. Lessens political pressure on aching callouses.
2. Prevents twisted ankle bracelets.
3. Reduces tendinitis, and in some cases, gingivitis.
4. Cuts down on the incidence of Hammer and Sickle toes.
5. Puts podiatrists out of work.

DISADVANTAGES OF AERO-PHOBICS

1. Results not immediate.
2. Can take up to 30 seconds for a man to be declared legally dead.
3. 15 seconds to be declared illegally dead.
4. Or 10 seconds, if he's a real prince, to be declared regally dead.

But what about the man who's uncomfortable about this kind of group atmosphere? Who would prefer not leaving the house because it would require help—from the entire U.S. Army Corps of Engineers—just to slip on his socks?

Well, luckily, there's an at-home exercise program that you can help supervise. It's easy. It's fun. And it's quite effective. Just make sure your man is completely relaxed and in comfortable clothes, with his life insurance paid up.

JANE FONDUE'S "AERO-PHOBIC" INSTRUCTIONS TO WOMEN

A. SAY THE FOLLOWING STATEMENTS SINCERELY TO YOUR MAN.
B. STAND THREE INCHES AWAY FROM HIM.
C. USE A MEGAPHONE.
D. REPEAT TILL HIS EKG IS FLATTER THAN KANSAS.

1. "My parents want to meet you."
2. "To tell you the truth, my last boyfriend was bisexual."
3. "Oh those weren't Dramamine, those were my birth control pills."
4. "I'm two months late."
5. "Gee. That's funny. My husband never gets home this early."
6. "I'm in love with you."
7. "I'm really in love with you!"
8. "Boy, am I in love with you!"
9. "How come you never say you love me?"
10. "Maybe tonight I could tie you up?"
11. "Honey, my whole family's coming over for dinner tonight. You'll just love them, cause they're the Manson family."
12. "That's not my G-spot. That's a spot on the carpet."

13. "Your wife and I had a very interesting talk this morning."
14. "So you have a boy who's eight, and a girl who's nine. That's wonderful. I'd like to meet them sometime and tell them how much their daddy loves water sports."
15. "Herpes. Syphilis. Gonorrhea. No, guess again."
16. "You're the best I've ever had. This week."

"My husband's name is Don. Perhaps you've heard of him? Don Corleone."

17. "Well, actually I'm fourteen."

As you can see from this varied menu, getting a conveniently placed blood vessel to burst in your man's cerebrum is more than a stroke of luck. It takes a certain degree of diligence and planning. All well and good. But at this point, even after you've enlisted your guy in an "Aero-phobics" program, there is probably still one nagging question that's uppermost in your mind.

So let us ask it for you:

"THIS IS ALL GREAT, JANE. BUT HOW DO I TELL MY MAN IS DEAD?"

It's simple. Just check the following symptoms and see whether he has any one, or all of them, for that matter. O.K. Your man is dead . . .

1. If the nurses and doctors start playing Pac-Man on his heart monitor.
2. If six weeks after eating in an expensive French restaurant, he still hasn't ordered dessert.
3. If during sex, he keeps on sliding off onto the floor.
4. If he begins to smell like downtown Calcutta.
5. If he appears unworried that his unemployment checks are coming to an end.
6. If he's so stiff that he can maintain erection but not a conversation.*
7. If, in the last six months, he hasn't urinated.
8. If he offers no resistance to cleaning the dishes. (This is perhaps the clearest sign of all—**author**.)
9. If he seems to be attracting an unusual number of flies.
10. If he's Benito Mussolini, Jimmy Hoffa, or if he's frequently mistaken for Ronald Reagan.
11. If his ghost appears and demands transfusions of ectoplasma.
12. If more than 90% of his body is covered with moss.
13. If he doesn't object to your mother staying for the month.

*Well, actually, this could indicate he's alive too.

14. If his expression seems almost unchanged after repeated stabbings.
15. If he doesn't whine that he's missing the football game while he's being buried.
16. If living with him isn't quite as bad as it used to be.

CHAPTER 16

THE HIGH-SUGAR/ LOW-ESTEEM DIET (OR HOW TO COOK YOUR MAN'S GOOSE)

Natural, healthy food—food that's high in vitamins, minerals and protein while remaining low in saturated fat—is obviously far too good for the creeps most women are involved with today.

As a matter of fact, in one recent survey, wives proclaimed that they would like nothing better than to see their husbands leave home and run off with a periodontist, unless they lived in France, where women preferred that their man run off with a "Perrier-dontist." No doubt, this attitude is further aggravated by the fact that the vast majority of French men are also "Sado-vegetarians" (sexual deviates who can only achieve orgasm after tying up their wives and then spanking a Waldorf salad).

Consequently, given the worldwide proliferation of fresh vegetables, lean roast beef, and breakfast cereals containing over 99.8% dietary fiber, it's small wonder that any woman in this day and age can provide her man with the essentials of a totally unbalanced diet.

Luckily, thanks to advances made just within the last three thousand years, all these gals have to do is remember one simple nutritional fact of life:

HYPOGLYCEMIA: HOW SWEET IT IS!

Two thirds of all Men Who Hate Themselves have low blood sugar (the other third has low blood saccharin). In medical terminology, this condition is known as hypoglycemia. Men afflicted with this ailment undergo incredible mood swings and some even become heroine addicts, experiencing an insatiable desire to stockpile the latest issues of *Supergirl* and *Wonder Woman* magazines. Others show more insidious symptoms and often become fixated on obscure films, such as *Steve Lawrence of Arabia*.

Of course, how can a man tell if he's hypoglycemic? In order to determine this, he must eat foods high in sugar and then see whether he has the following symptoms: migraines, fatigue, irritability, plus the inability to say the word "fructose" in the presence of dwarfs.

Salvadore Lovehandle has survived for the past thirty-six years on a diet that consists entirely of omelets and soufflés made from chocolate eggs, occasionally garnished with sprigs of licorice. Yet not only has he found the time to be nervous, exhausted and overweight, but he's also been able to become emotionally and physically involved with a Milky Way bar, whom he simply calls his little "Sugar."

Of course, Salvadore is one of the more obvious hypoglycemics. The question is, how can a Man Who Hates Himself tell whether or not he's one too? Fortunately, it's quite simple. Just make sure he answers the following questions yes or no.

1. Do you find that a Ring Ding is the most perfect object in the universe? (With the possible exception of Bo Derek clad only in 100% pure cotton candy.)

2. Would you be willing to "seek out and destroy" any foreign power that threatened to cut off America's vital supply of Oreos?

3. Over the fireplace, do you have mounted the trophy of a chocolate mousse?

4. Every eight hours, for symptomatic relief, must you take two capsules of time-release nougat?

5. Have you ever requested papal dispensation to wed your Twinkie?

Any Man Who Hates Himself, even if he had only one yes answer, should stop whatever he's doing and immediately start pan-broiling a Nestle's Crunch bar. However, even a Man Who Hates Himself will have occasional lapses and attempt to eat food that's healthy and nutritious.

Hypoglycemic being disciplined with a sugar cane

This is the time when The Woman Who Truly Hates Him must step in and take charge of the situation. Let him know, quite firmly, you intend to make sure that he sticks to the following dietary plan. What's more, you should remind him that if he ever has a wholesome meal again you'll have no choice but to discipline him quite severely—with a sugar cane!

IF HE WANTS	GIVE HIM
1. Scallops champignon; tuna casserole; clams on the half shell	1. A herring marinated in Bosco (or a Clark bar in white clam sauce)
2. Beef Wellington; filet mignon; quarter-pound cheeseburgers	2. An ox basted with maple syrup in a bed of Hershey's Kisses
3. Baked ziti; fettucini Alfredo; chicken Tetrazzini	3. Angel's hair pasta in creamery glucose; ravioli à la Milk Duds; veal parmesan drenched with molasses
4. Orange, grapefruit, or prune juice	4. A hogshead of Kool-Aid immediately followed by a vat of vanilla fudge borscht
5. Steamed mussels in white wine and garlic	5. Steamed M&Ms in white wine and garlic
6. Grinders; sloppy joes; hero sandwiches	6. A peanut-butter and Jell-O sandwich, topped off by a honey-glazed hoagie
7. Lamb tikka; bhuna gosht	7. Tandoori marshmallows; curried cannolis with chutney
8. Cocaine	8. Opiated marzipan

9. Chicken teriyaki; futo maki; yakitori

9. Freshly sliced tuna and jelly roll, served with a choice of brownie tempura or chocolate-chip sushi

10. Matzo brei

10. Gefilte glacé

11. Chili con carne; hot tamales; burritos

11. Enchiladas stuffed with halvah; refried Tootsie Rolls

12. Peking duck; beef lo mein; mooshu pork

12. Hot-and-sour strudel; stir-fried chicken with Reese's Pieces

MEN WHO HATE THEMSELVES:
BY FAVORITE FOOD

Barbecued chicken	04%
Waffles with ice cream	03.9%
Beets	97%
Tuna in water	97.1%
Lasagna	.000000063%
Meat ravioli	.000000062%
Cheese ravioli	.000000061%
Pizza (with mushrooms)	.0000000000000009%
Broccoli	98.6%
Sushi (deluxe platter)	34%
Sushi (regular)	27%
Sushi (à la carte)	23%
Low-fat cottage cheese	89%
TV dinners	107.92%
Roast duck au Grand Marnier	02.35%
Lox, bagels & cream cheese	02.35%
Grapefruit	99.999999999%
Turkey on rye	68%
String beans	81.89%
Protein toast	89.81%
Pepto-bismol shakes	90007.16%
Hoagies	52%

CHAPTER 17

ZEN AND THE ART OF ANTIPATHY

"A rose by any other name still wilts."

—GUNGA GLICK*

Scientists at the University of Miami have recently discovered, after fourteen years of research, conclusive new evidence of Death after Life. This should come as no surprise to Men Who Hate Themselves, those such as Ned Foyeur. For he is a spiritual being. A beliver in the ultimate power and supreme force that rules over the entire cosmos, also known, in some circles, as the IRS. Here is how his ex-girlfriend Roz Niche tells it.

KARMA AND THE DELI LAMA

"Jed was strictly into karma. That's Karma Miranda, the famous Tibetan nightclub singer. He would go out every night and try to catch glimpses of her at this one downtown restaurant, called the Deli Lama. Strange place. To

*Yogi, raconteur, and former coat tree at the Iranian embassy.

work there you would have to produce a résumé that gave all the employment experience you ever had, including the jobs you held in previous lifetimes, plus references.

"All right, all right, back to Jeff. Sure he was weird, but I have to admit that I couldn't help admiring a guy who had built up over 380,000 frequent flyer miles, yeah, and all of those were on astral planes. That's right. He was a very picky traveler, always insisting on booking special flights that would only carry him to predestinations.

"You know, we just didn't seem to have anything in common anymore, and, toward the end, he went out and became a Jewish Buddhist. He claimed that it was the only holistic way of purifying the body and dry-cleaning the soul, but I had my doubts.

"As I recall, the last time I ever saw him he was sitting cross-legged in the living room, smoking opiated tofu, while chanting, 'Hare Knishna Hare Knisha/Cherry Knishna Potato Knishna/Hare Bagel Hare Bagel/Toasted Bagel Cream Cheese Bagel.' Well, I think you get the picture."

Jewish Buddhist

A PROFOUND AND MYSTICAL STATE OF DECAY

Keeping the previous case study in mind, our research has shown that Men Who Hate Themselves are obsessed by trying to achieve that profound and mystical state of decay that occurs only after hundreds of LSD trips, thousands of mescaline trips, or one trip to Cleveland.

All over the country, they're attempting to unite the wisdom of the ancient Zen masters with the knowledge of Donald Trump for the purpose of creating a space—and then subletting it.

A Case of Mind-Contraction

"I started getting into mind-contracting techniques in the late 60's. At that time, the movement that was the most popular was past (Please Stifle Thought). After sixty hours without sleep, the one thing that I remember was the trainers encouraging us to get off this life/death wheel of karma and instead, maybe have a Pepsi.

"After that experience, I decided to probe the very boundaries of Cosmic Unconsciousness itself—but I eventually gave up, after coming to the music of Barry Manilow."

SWAMI BABA GANOUSCH

For centuries, Men Who Hate Themselves have been journeying to the temple of the Master himself, Swami Baba Ganousch, in order to absorb his teachings, while at the same time getting away from their wives for the weekend.

You see, from his shrine high above the River Ganges, the Almighty Seer has proclaimed that what awaits each and every one of his disciples is nothing less than Universal Redemption, providing they've also been saving green stamps.

To illustrate this point more clearly to Men Who Hate Themselves, the Swami frequently tells a series of parables. Strict adherence to the principles contained within each one, he says confidently, shall produce a wondrous sense of being reborn. For a few men, however, this may occur inside the original womb.

Parable #1

A simple woodsman of Braman falls asleep. But while he slumbers, his consciousness is suddenly projected up to the ceiling. Looking down at the miserable body of the woodsman, and the miserable body of the woodsman's wife, it thinks better of the arrangement and decides to board a Greyhound bus to Philadelphia.

There it runs for office and becomes mayor and, after that, a shrimp appetizer at Arthur Treacher's. Six years come to pass and, all of a sudden, the woodsman wakes up in a panic, his forehead drenched in cold beads of tartar sauce.

Looking around his modest hut, he steadies his nerves and promises his wife that he will never again read any more books on Astral Rejection.

Parable #2

A good physician of Sutra who was old and wise, conversant with the medical arts, and skillful in defrauding Medicare, came home to find that his wife, by accident, had taken a poisonous substance. "Oh Blessed One!" he intoned. "Ask of me whatsoever you wish, but save the one I cherish!"

His prayers were soon answered and his wife died, allowing him to keep a date with his girlfriend Debbie, a computer programmer at the local Sheraton.

But later, as she whispered in his ear, "Let me program your software," the spirit of the physician's dead wife appeared in the form of a giant she-elephant, wearing a pants suit.

Stricken with remorse, the good physician fell to his knees and begged for mercy. But the elephant felt no pity for the two lovers and used all her great weight to crush them both to death, though she did resolve, later that week, to go on the Cambridge diet.

"As you can see," says the Swami in the most profound of tones, "life is a blind date with destiny." He then tells all the assembled Men Who Hate Themselves that, to complete their spiritual training, they must make a sacred vow to keep the following zen concepts in their hearts and minds for the rest of their lives, or through the end of the TV season, whichever comes first.

THE SACRED TEN OF ZEN FOR MEN

1. **SCHMATA:** A legendary Hindu garment that bestowed immortality, and a small rash, on the bearer.

2. **BENIHAHA:** The twenty-eighth patriarch of India and the first man to achieve Nirvana by doublecrossing a loanshark.

3. **LALA:** The void, the ocean of death, the realm of transitory existence, also known as Malibu.

4. **SARTRA:** A strange existential nausea, said to signal plagues, pestilence, or news of a paternity suit.

5. **NOOKA:** In Buddhist theology, the state of being where eternal oneness is achieved—with Jimmy Hoffa.

6. **ZITZBLAH:** A joyous philosophy; revelation itself; sacred knowledge based on the eternal truths of *The Beverly Hillbillies.*

7. **HELLA:**   After death, a state of misery and eternal anguish, reserved for licensed orthodontists.

8. **KOLA:**   A holy beverage; said to be made from Reincarnation Evaporated Milk.

9. **SHABAAS:**   A three-day religious holiday, celebrating a disciple's long ascent to cosmic perfection, ending with the traditional sacrifice of a literary agent.

10. **TEENA:**   A goddess of ancient Burma; the giver of eternal knowledge and, occasionally, a venereal disease.

CHAPTER 18

MEN LEARNING TO LOVE TO HATE THEMSELVES

- Peter, a male secretary, can stereotype over sixty people a minute.
- Mike, a casting agent, specializes in casting iron, fishing rods, and doubts.
- Jim, a professional flagpole sitter, feels inadequate because he can never apologize for being sorry.
- Harvey, a jockey, cries himself to sleep ever since his stable relationship broke up, and his beloved left him for a stud who more closely resembled Seattle Slew.
- David, an advertising creative director who earns over $365,000 a year, or $1,000 a day, was fired when he demanded an extra $1,000 during leap year.

Now what do these men all have in common?

Not that they hate themselves, but that they hate themselves for hating themselves. It's a universal dilemma. Yet even more disturbing is that there are men who have hated themselves all their lives but, for no apparent reason, suddenly begin to like themselves and yes, on rare occasions, even love themselves.

The end of a stable relationship

Obviously, these alien thoughts of self-worth are causing more than a few men consternation and fear. Without proper treatment, these individuals wind up with obsessive feelings of confidence and self-respect so severe that they may never again punish themselves by watching *Dating Game* reruns.

WHAT CAN BE DONE TO RESOLVE THIS NATIONAL PROBLEM?

"It's not easy," says Cleo Boz-Scagglia, Director of the American Institute for Self-Negation. "For most men live in states of quiet jubilation. Over and over again, these guys never stop complaining that they are condemned to live out the rest of their lives in total rapture, knowing only joy, harmony, and the ravages of utter bliss!"

As a professional, objective therapist, Dr. Boz-Scagglia is

determined to help men across the country get to the uncon-
scious roots of their happiness. "I believe these feelings of
ceaseless elation can be controlled," she said in a recent
article. "If not completely eliminated."

Cleo goes on to say that, in many ways, men are probably
just as cheerful as their prehistoric ancestors. But where
these Neanderthals were complacent, today's Neanderthals
take the pursuit of misery in dead earnest. She says ask any
man and he'll tell you, loud and clear, that he deserves far
worse than what he's got.

"But are men really doing everything in their power to
make their lives completely unbearable?" asks Dr. Boz-
Scagglia. "Probably not." She goes on to say that, in each
and every day of their lives, men are given golden opportuni-
ties to fail, but do they take advantage of them?

"I think the answer is pretty obvious."

At the American Institute for Self-Negation, Cleo Boz-
Scagglia and other dedicated women help men from all
walks of life achieve the despair and self-hatred they con-
stantly dream of. In the following dialogue, Dr. Boz-Scagglia
demonstrates just how.

Leo Wrestles with His Sense of Adequacy

LEO: I don't understand it. I seem to derive complete satisfaction from even the most mundane things I do in day-to-
day life. It's unnerving.

CLEO: Many men have the same complaint. Instead of
building yourself up, knock yourself down. Say to yourself, "What did I do wrong today? How did I foul up?"
Come on. You've lived for over forty-five years. It's time to
stop acting like an adult.

LEO: I want to! I want to! More than anything else, I want
that spoiled, erratic, sadistic child that I know is just
under the surface to come out and be heard. But he never

does. Day in and day out, I just go on, performing open heart surgery, winning awards and the respect of the entire medical community.

CLEO: It's not as bleak as it seems. The trouble is you never really wanted to fail. That's right. The time is now, before you do something that you'll actually be proud of, to screw up.

LEO: Don't you think I've tried? I go in and scrub down. The nurse wipes the perspiration from my forehead. She slaps the scalpel in my hand. I know what I have to do. But then I lose my nerve and the operation is a success.

CLEO: Relax a little. Who says every patient has to pull through? Or any of them, for that matter?

LEO: What can I do? No matter what, I'm always stuck with these good feelings about myself.

CLEO: Really, it's nothing to be ashamed of. We are finding more and more men, with even less justification than yourself, who are willing to admit that they have a positive self-image.

LEO: I guess the problem really is . . . I'm not an alcoholic.

CLEO: Unfortunately, that's a pattern we're seeing more frequently, especially amongst teenage boys who don't drink. Have you thought about joining SA (Sobriety Anonymous)? There, with group support, patience, and understanding, even a Nobel Prize-winner like yourself, in six months, can be turned into a useless derelict with a bad liver.

LEO: If only I could believe that! I suppose, when you examine all the issues, I just never was able to overcome the effects of a good childhood. Is it possible, somehow, that this can be changed?

CLEO: Yes, but it's difficult. Being healthy and well-adjusted is a burden that many of us carry all our lives. We are tolerant and patient, loving and compassionate. As a result of that, we have many close friends and rewarding, stimulating careers.

LEO: Small wonder that we can manage at all.

CLEO: Exactly.

LEO: So you're saying that it was all our parents' fault?

CLEO: Precisely.

LEO: But wouldn't it be better just to forget all the wonderful things they did for us?

CLEO: No, that would be the worst thing.

LEO: It's so difficult. I mean, remembering how they took care of me when I was sick. The nights they lent me the car. All the times they said they loved me.

CLEO: That's right. They're the reason you function so well.

LEO: When I think of it I could . . . could . . . mur . . .

CLEO: Good. Take that resentment and transfer it to your present relationships.

LEO: Even work?

CLEO: Of course.

LEO: But suppose I get a promotion. Suppose they want to make me president of the A.M.A.

CLEO: Don't take it! You're not worthy. If anything, your license should have been revoked long ago. You're incompetent! Do you hear me!? A wretched blob of inarticulate protoplasm!!

LEO: That's an exciting and lovely thought. I would love to hold onto that forever. But just when I'm getting things untogether, I get these horrible feelings of peace and certainty.

CLEO: Then add some chaos to your life. Listen closely and always remember this—you can't cope! You never could and you never will!

LEO: Sure. Sure. That's easy to say. But life is so fair.

CLEO: Then think of the inequities, the injustices, the incredible cruelties that men have inflicted upon each other, and on women too, throughout the centuries!

LEO: Please, don't stop.

CLEO: The massacres, the inquisitions, the fiendish tortures, add them up and you get the senseless slaughter of countless billions of innocent people!!

LEO: Wow! Fabulous! Already I feel much worse. Is there any way that I can ever thank you?

CLEO: Kill yourself.

Thanks to Dr. Boz-Scagglia's efforts, Leo was able to enter into a horrendous relationship with a woman who was a *real* New Yorker. It was tragic. For seven years they tried to have a baby but couldn't, because it turned out her eggs were hard-boiled. On the plus side, she did teach him that having casual sex didn't necessarily entail having to wear a leisure suit.

A few weeks after the affair had ended, and on the advice of Dr. Boz-Scagglia, Leo quit his job and ventured straight out to Hollywood where, because of his looks, he was immediately offered an incredible film deal. That's right. An incredible film deal! Twenty-five percent off a roll of Kodak.

Men like Leo, who are interested in additional advice from Dr. Boz-Scagglia, should consult her next book, *The Art of Loathing*. Or, for those more impatient, dial 1-800-HATE MEN.*

*Nothing will happen, but please keep trying.

ABOUT THE AUTHOR

Born out of gridlock, in the backseat of a taxicab, Mr. Rudnitsky shares his birthdate with Helen Keller and Attila the Hun, explaining why so many of his contemporaries consider him a deaf mute barbarian. During his early years, his mother diligently attended to the household and, by age 32, he no longer needed to be breastfed and was allowed to venture anywhere, so long as it didn't involve crossing the street.

Mr. Rudnitsky (that's Rud-Niet-Ski, Russian for condominium) is a popular figure at seminars and lectures, and his notorious sense of humor has been known to provoke audiences, across the country, to near riotous states of total absence. Even at family gatherings relatives often force him to dodge questions—and occasionally a brick. On the plus side, close associates find him a modest, unaffected person who likes to sit around and chew the fat or, if the gal is close enough, the cellulite.

In real life, Rudnitsky is a Creative Director at one of the largest advertising agencies in all of Sri Lanka. Ask anyone in the business and they'll immediately tell you that his numerous commercials have electrified millions upon millions —of bacteria on TV screens from coast to coast.

Currently, the author is hard at work on an inspirational new work that will encourage Americans everywhere to give up their dreary nine-to-five jobs and instead lead the exciting fast-paced life of a writer of humor books. Look for it—*Poverty Without Risk*—at your local bookstore, or, if it's not available there, try your local landfill.